DEATH BY APPOINTMENT

A DR CATHY MORELAND MYSTERY #BOOK ONE

MAIRI CHONG

BLOODHOUND
— BOOKS —

www.bloodhoundbooks.com

Print ISBN 978-1-914614-62-0

For W – More than anything

1

1990

The boys shouldn't have been at Devil's Leap that morning. It was only because of Kevin MacDonald and his lies they had come at all. The excursion was forbidden. Everyone knew you didn't go down there. It had always been so, for generations. But they had gone all the same. It had been called Devil's Leap for as long as anyone could remember, although few residents of Kinnaven could tell you why. Following that dreadful day, however, no one could deny the name's suitability.

Kevin had been full of it on the last day of term. Some of the boys sat on him and told him he wouldn't get to go in goal for the whole of lunch break if he didn't come up with the goods. Still, he had drawn it out. Kevin was always doing that. The older boys said he was a bit thick because his dad hit him about, and then there was Kevin's mother, of course. But this time, despite their misgivings, the brothers had listened with the rest of the crowd, gathered around Kevin on the playing fields before the bell went.

Across and to the left of the first tombstone, he had told them all. He even went on to say he had climbed right down, but that was absolute nonsense. Everybody knew it was impossible. But Kevin always was a fibber. Most of the boys had given it up after that, realising that it was just another of his stories. But the brothers were determined to look for themselves. They had their return to school after the summer holidays in mind, armed with a tale to tell, yet again outing Kevin as a liar.

The eldest boy now led the way, hopping and stumbling over the dew-soaked scrubland, his brother trotting breathlessly behind. They had lain the bike reverently at the beginning of the moor, forced to continue on foot. Although it had caused countless disagreements already, it was still a much-prized possession. The youngest had been begging for a Raleigh Styler for ages, and when it was finally presented to him the previous week for his birthday, it did not disappoint. The gift had been given on the stipulation that it was for sharing and the seat should be adjusted to his older brother's height, hence the quarrel. Unfortunately, the seat itself was not large enough for two, but that morning, perched and wobbling with one on the seat and the other balanced on the trick pegs, they had set out before the sun reached the windowsills of the sleeping hamlet.

The air that morning was fresh and brought with it a fine mist that settled casually on the boys' skin. The eldest noticed and licked his upper lip, tasting the salt, checking for the bristle that he wished was there, but was not.

The tide was at its lowest now, and the shore lay beaten following the sea's torments overnight. Two large rocks, almost half the height of the cliff itself, protruded from the water's edge. Two craggy tombstones. Fuelled by arrogance, the sea raced between them, smashing with a frothy spume in conceited glory. The rocks remained unmoved.

The oldest boy stood close to the edge, his hand-me-down plimsolls saturated, his shorts and T-shirt billowing in the breeze like a sail. He leaned out, searching for the promised cave, hoping also, perhaps, to spot a hidden nook for treasure, having just seen *Shipwrecked* at the cinema the previous week for his brother's birthday treat. Since seeing the film, the two had spoken of little else and, despite their parents' protestations that no sharks or treasure would be found off the east coast of Scotland, they lived in hope. The boy leaned further but saw nothing. His brother, by far the more foolhardy, suddenly jostled past, and with a shout of excitement, began the descent.

The path was overgrown and at times the boys had to crouch and shuffle, grabbing for the heather and seagrasses by the side. The earth beneath their feet crunched and slid. Pebbles came loose and rained down, thundering over the edge like hail and bullets.

Finally, they paused, breathless and panting, their progress prevented by the end of the path and marked by a wrought-iron bench. The youngest boy climbed up and stood on the metal seat, entwined with golden gorse and a mass of fiery willowherb. The bench had, at one time, been painted a dark green but was now splintered and bubbled, damaged by salt, sun and wind. No one had been down this far for years.

From his elevated position, the boy squinted, searching to the left of the first huge rock for any sign of the supposed cave. In truth, although he wished Kevin to be wrong, he more dearly longed to discover the cave himself. He saw none, but caught sight of something else almost immediately, distinguishing it from the rocky shadows in the early-morning light. A chill of revulsion spread over him. He gasped and fell against his older brother. Together they huddled against the cliff, unable to move.

As the sun rose and the bodies of a woman and her newborn child were lifted, the rest of Kinnaven slowly began to stir. None of its residents could know that for years to come, the tragedy would fester. The minister said that, given the opportunity, wounds would heal, but he was wrong. In this case, the sore would seep and necrose. Over the years, suffering would pass stealthily through the village streets, along Monduff Wynd and Shore Road, up to the decaying farm where an old farmer once sat, talking of bygone days, his face as weathered and furrowed as the land on which his father, and his before him, had farmed. The sorrow might, for the most part, go unnoticed, but would ultimately culminate in bitterness and malevolence as cruel as the sea itself.

2

2020

Dr Cathy Moreland gazed out of the barred hospital window. Best not get up again. They didn't like it the last time. She'd only been trying to look at the sky. A muscular man in corduroy trousers had walked briskly across and raised an arm. Ridiculous. Like some kind of absurd barrier. She had held his gaze for a moment or two. Then, smiling, she had returned to her seat. She imagined they were being extra cautious given who she was.

The trees in the distance acted as a buffer between sky and land. She watched their tops catch, heavy in the wind. The leaves fluttered and changed. What a waste of a day being stuck there when outside seemed infinitely more favourable.

She turned and frowned at her interrogator. He, along with the corduroys, were seated a small distance from her. She must have been asked a question. Both were looking expectantly at her.

'Well...' she said, and left it at that, lolling defiantly against the low, foam chair, the back of which was encased in a hideous carpet material. She grinned and waited.

Her interrogator removed his glasses and sighed. He was, she supposed, nearing retirement. Dressed smartly as one might expect, in a suit and, much to her amusement, a waistcoat of muted floral pattern. He looked every bit the part. His face showed great strength, with a high forehead and intelligent, if not shrewd, eyes. His jaw was firm, but occasionally, if one looked closely, and Cathy had, his muscles relaxed and gave a more good-natured set to his mouth. He was tall and his movements were deliberate and easy. She supposed he must have been quite striking as a younger man. He had been called in specially to see her, she expected.

'Bipolar disorder,' he said with a note of caution.

Cathy beamed. She couldn't help it. 'I know,' she said, feeling the delight of a child at their cleverness. 'What are we thinking then? Lithium?'

The psychiatric consultant smiled wanly and continued to scratch notes in his pad. Cathy's slender hands twitched. She wished she could snatch the paper from him and read what he had said. His hand continued to move across the page.

'I'm not sure I'm keen on lithium,' Cathy said, snapping her gaze from his writing and allowing her eyes to wander out and across the skyline once more. 'I know you'll make me take something, of course.' She turned sharply to look at him, almost daring him to disagree. He remained impassive, though. 'Did the antidepressants push me over the edge then?'

She had slept little and eaten even less over the last few days. The hours had merged. Strangely though, she had still felt an exhausting dynamism, as if her mind was working at twice, if not three times, its usual speed. He was answering her and she would need to concentrate again. What a bore it all was.

'The antidepressants may not have helped,' he said, closing the cardboard folder containing her case notes. 'They've elevated your mood certainly, but you've become hypomanic now, as you are no doubt aware. It was always a risk. Your initial presentation was ambiguous, to say the least. A mild to moderate anxiety state, we thought, as you know. I had hoped the time off might be enough, along with the medication, but then, of course, there have been other elements altering your mental well-being. The alcohol, the prescription drugs. Work also, the rigours of which were outwith your control, as we've discussed.'

Cathy snorted and bounced her leg back and forth repeatedly. The consultant watched but said nothing, his pen resting now on the closed file.

The room grew darker as clouds covered the sun. She wondered when this would end. She could reach out now to those creamy, claustrophobic walls and push. Push with all her might, plunging her hands through the boarded plaster and paint, splintering the wood until she was able to breathe. She glanced again at the corduroys and wondered if she had enough speed and dexterity to make a dive for the door.

The man in corduroys, seeming to realise her thoughts, shifted. 'I think...' he began.

The suited consultant turned and nodded. 'Yes, of course,' he replied to the unsaid sentiment.

In desperation, she called out as the psychiatrist began to get up. She almost begged. Her voice was shrill and not her own.

It was the first time she had shown any appropriate emotion, and even to him, an experienced and hardened practitioner, the distress must have been stirring. He looked down at her now, seeing the lank hair hanging about her pale face. Her wide-set, intelligent eyes reflected the sliver of strip light. Below them, the skin looked fragile, almost bruised.

'Stress probably caused it,' he said simply. This was not the time or the place to go into it further. There would be plenty of opportunities to discuss the whys and wherefores over the coming days once the medication had begun to kick in.

She grimaced. Stress. What kind of reason was that? Cathy inspected her fingers, smoothing the skin around her bitten nails. 'Stress,' she whispered under her breath a couple of times and then grabbing the edge of her seat, she leaned forward.

'Stress!' she screamed and then fell back in hysterical laughter.

The man was already halfway to the door. The only sign he showed of unease was a slight hesitation in his step, but he did not turn. Instead, the corduroys came towards her as she knew they must.

Hand on the doorknob, the consultant paused. 'We'll start you on the medication, Dr Moreland.' Even though she was near hysteria, she recognised the unmistakable sadness in his voice. 'You'll stay in with us until you're stabilised, if you have no objection. I'm sure in a few days, you'll be a good deal more like yourself. I'll check in on you tomorrow and see how you're doing.'

When he was gone, she wept. Hot, embittered, childish tears. Her face stung and she wiped at her cheeks with the sleeve of her blouse. She drew her knees up to her chest and hugged them to her. 'Oh God, why?' she mouthed, but no sound came.

Fingers brushed her arm. The corduroys were standing beside her now. She looked up blindly.

'He's written you up for aripiprazole,' the trousers said. 'It'll be easier than lithium. I've seen a good few patients respond well and it works fast. We'll start you on it now.'

Cathy nodded, but she knew it was over. Her life as a doctor was at an end, and therefore everything was done.

~

The days in the hospital passed in a blur. People came and went, including the consultant, just as he had promised. She nodded and held her hands clasped tightly together in an attempt to hide their movement. She ate when she was told to, and took her medication as instructed, observed all the while by corduroys or another of the nursing team. Much of her day was spent gazing out of one of the tall windows. More often than not, she could be found on the second-floor landing, a chair pulled close to the wide radiator that clunked into action at exactly eight thirty in the morning and again at five thirty at night. From this position, she could look out at the grounds, the hospital being set within possibly a five-acre plot, much of which was lawned and lined by trees. Paths of dark-grey quarry dust intersected the buildings dotted about the grounds. All were surrounded by a high wall. Sometimes people came and went, their figures looked small from where she sat, but snatches of their chatter occasionally carried on the breeze up to her and through the single glazing. She listened dispassionately, too tired to make any sense of it, too broken to care.

She had seen it all before, having worked in a similar hospital for her mental health rotation. As a doctor, of course, one was surrounded by safety. There were panic buttons and buzzer systems, there were muscular, male nurses ready to step in. Finally, as a doctor, one might leave at the end of the day, or at any time, for that matter. The exit would have a four- or five-digit code. She would have been able to key this in, glancing around to make sure she was safe to do so, and then swinging the heavy door open enough to move through, she would await the springs to draw back into position and slam safely shut again. Cathy hadn't considered absconding, not since that first day. The medication had calmed her. It had appeased those ideas at least. She would ride it out. She knew this was ultimately the most effective way to be discharged.

'You look bloody awful,' Suzalinna said, a week after she had been admitted.

Cathy was seated by the window and her friend pulled over a chair to join her. By this time, she had been deemed safe enough and adequately normal to take visitors. Suzalinna had arrived and had suggested they get out of the ward and go for a walk around the grounds, but Cathy shook her head.

'They've said it's all right, you know,' Suzalinna had urged. 'If we stick to the main gardens and around the south buildings. I've asked already.'

'Maybe later. I don't feel like walking just now.' She turned to look out of the window once more. They had known one another since medical school and Suzalinna had been a much-trusted friend over the years, not least standing by Cathy recently, during the decline in her mental health. It was Suzalinna and her husband, Saj, who had originally driven her to the hospital to be assessed, both knowing their friend could no longer go on self-medicating with alcohol and low-dose opiates in an attempt to soothe her elevated mood. Cathy and Suzalinna were opposites in many respects. Cathy had found it hard to settle into her chosen career in general practice. Her friend had known exactly what she wanted to be from the start. Suzalinna had been a consultant in accident and emergency medicine long before many of her peers had even gained their status as registrar. She was ambitious and determined, sometimes, Cathy thought, a little ruthless also. But despite their differences, Suzalinna's near arrogance and Cathy's more malleable approach seemed to gel and arguments between the two medics were rare.

'I thought you'd be desperate to get outside,' Suzalinna went on, absent-mindedly folding the straps of her handbag around and around. 'Bloody awful being stuck in here with all of this going on.' Her friend gestured as the man who Cathy now knew as Crazy George, ambled by, genuflecting at the ceiling and muttering about God's will, as often he did when visitors came to the ward. Cathy smiled.

'You'd think, wouldn't you?' she said.

Suzalinna seemed disconcerted. 'Well, darling, what have they said to you? Are they pleased with how things are going? I spoke to Dr Christie on the phone the other day. I know he can't breach confidentiality and all that nonsense, but he seems optimistic.'

Cathy raised her eyebrows. She watched a man being led across the lawn to the building she now knew housed the art department and workshops, a type of therapy encouraged for the long-term patients.

Suzalinna leaned forward. 'Cath, for Christ sakes,' her friend hissed.

Cathy turned and looked at her sadly.

'What the hell's going on?' Suzalinna asked. 'You're getting home in a few days. I know they've told you that. One of the nurses said to me at the door. Aren't you pleased? They think you'll make a good recovery. You'll be on the tablets for the foreseeable future, but otherwise, you're good to go.' Suzalinna shook her head in disbelief. 'I don't understand...'

Cathy blinked and looked out at the trees in the distance. They sat in silence.

'Listen, darling,' Suzalinna finally said. 'Saj and I have been talking about what happens after you're discharged. I know you're worrying about work and about when you can go back. I want you to forget about that now, okay? It'll happen for sure if you want it to, but you need to give it time.'

Cathy continued to stare out of the window.

'You can come and stay with us for a bit until you're more

like yourself,' Suzalinna went on. 'Perhaps we could get away together for a while. I've got annual leave coming up. Maybe we could take a girly trip. Remember the elective way up north, in our final year? That crazy medical placement? It'd be like old times. What do you think? Back to Kinnaven for a bit of nostalgia? I could book a cottage. It'd be just the place to start your recovery. All that beautiful, wild Scottish scenery and the fresh sea air. Where better than the north-east, where the dialect is unintelligible and everyone is married to their cousin?'

Despite herself, a smile pricked the corners of Cathy's lips.

3

The letters had begun the week before. The elderly GP initially thought they were either a mistake or a practical joke. The first two had been particularly cryptic. By the third, though, old Dr Cosgrove knew their meaning. She could almost predict what the following one might say. They spelt out a date that she remembered only too well. Vicious and cruel to bring it up again. And why now? With what purpose?

They had arrived by post. All had come in the same style of small white envelope with the address scrawled in blue ink. It looked like an elderly person's writing, but Dr Cosgrove believed this was an amateurish attempt to disguise the actual hand. She hadn't noticed the postmark on the first, but the last two had had an Aberdeen stamp. That hardly narrowed things down, though. Kinnaven was north of Aberdeen and the city was where most of its inhabitants did their 'big shop'. She felt sure the culprit must be a Kinnaven resident.

She wondered if she should talk to someone. What would she say, though? The letters were hardly threatening and, to anyone else, they would be meaningless. Still, she wished she had someone in whom she could confide. She thought of Ruth, her practice partner, but almost immediately ruled this idea out. She had enough on her plate with the new salaried GP and thoughts of her, Dr Cosgrove's, impending retirement. There was, of course, the minister. She shook her head. No, she couldn't abide the idea. If only her father had been alive, or her mother, for that matter. It was a long time since she had been to the graveyard in Aberdeen to lay flowers.

Dr Cosgrove looked at her computer screen and saw that the next patient was in. At least at work, she felt safe. The letters had only been delivered to her home address. This, she thought, had been quite deliberate. It made them more personal. Dr Cosgrove sighed. The perpetrator might tire of the silly little game soon enough. She had suffered far worse when she first arrived in the village. The residents were a tough crowd to please. Stuck in their ways and wary of a strange face. Now, she was accepted. Yes, of course. If another letter came, she would toss it in the bin and think no more about it.

Dr Cosgrove removed her glasses and rubbed the bridge of her nose, indented by their weight.

She had been the lead clinician for what seemed like a lifetime. Both her parents had been general practitioners, and the idea of any other specialty seemed highly unlikely for her. As a student, she had fleetingly toyed with the notion of a career in ophthalmology but was quickly dissuaded. Her father had been instrumental in negotiating, and financially securing, the practice. Unfortunately for the newly established young Dr Cosgrove, her father's interest was not purely financial and for the first few years, he was an ever-officious presence.

But things had changed since those early days. Dr Cosgrove's practice was no longer single-handed, and she had grown in confidence and skill. She had taken on a full-time partner eleven years before as the area population had grown. It had been an excellent decision. Ruth was quiet and capable.

When Ruth knocked on her door later that morning, Dr Cosgrove's thoughts were no longer on the anonymous letters and she was quite consumed with practice business once again.

'All quiet?' Ruth asked.

'All quiet. For now, anyway. Come in, Ruth, and speak. Shut the door.'

Ruth entered the room and, knowing Dr Cosgrove well, flopped on a seat, folding a leg under her. 'Anything interesting today then? Anyone actually ill?'

Doctor Cosgrove smiled at her colleague.

They spoke of a couple of patients. Ruth had received some abnormal blood results for one of the elderly patients Dr Cosgrove usually saw, and Dr Cosgrove told her about the death of one of their palliative care cases, a gentleman with lung cancer.

'Not wholly unexpected,' her partner said, and Dr Cosgrove nodded. 'And how are you feeling about things?' Ruth asked. 'I've been meaning to come in and talk all this week, Heather.'

'The retirement, you mean? Oh fine,' Dr Cosgrove said as she gazed out of her window again. It had begun to drizzle and she watched as the droplets of rain touched the pane and slowly made their descent, collecting and merging. 'I think the salaried girl has been the right decision, don't you?' She smiled at Ruth. 'She's mopping up most of the house calls, I see, and did you notice how busy it was last Monday? She made no fuss or nonsense though. Just got on with things. Where has she come from? Isn't she an Edinburgh graduate?'

'Yes, she's still based there, I believe.' Ruth had picked up one of Dr Cosgrove's neatly arranged pens and turned it over to read the name of the pharmaceutical company that had sponsored it. 'I think her boyfriend's looking for work up here too now. She was saying they're hoping to move permanently. She's been house-hunting apparently.'

'She's serious about staying around then? The commute must be dreadful.' Dr Cosgrove leaned back in her swivel chair. She did so enjoy these times to talk. They were usually so busy, and inevitably, one of the reception girls would be hounding them for a prescription or to take a phone call. *We must make more time for these chats*, Dr Cosgrove thought.

'I think she's got a friend close by who she's staying with during the week. Anyway, we'll see how she goes.' Ruth paused and looked at her partner acutely. 'What do you think about her as partnership material when you go?'

The question was a hard slap in the face. She almost physically recoiled. Afterwards, she reflected on her stupidity. Of course, Ruth would look to take on a new partner when she retired. Salaried GPs were all very well short term, but if you wanted commitment and longevity, a partnership was always the way to go. The thought of being replaced though, and in the practice she had built up from scratch, was not a pleasant one.

Ruth's expression had changed. When had her partner's admiration turned into pity?

Dr Cosgrove smiled brightly. 'I think she'd be excellent, Ruth. Yes. Excellent.'

Dr Cosgrove did not join her staff for coffee that morning. Since she had started the Kinnaven practice, there had been a tradition. It had been instigated by one of the original girls who had since retired. She had been a wonderful find. Dedicated to her work and devoted to Dr Cosgrove herself. She had known the true meaning of looking after the doctor, keeping patients' requests to a minimum and allowing only the seriously unwell to make an appointment. But her care had not stopped there. Every Friday, a cake would be placed on the front desk. A gift to her. Dr Cosgrove had, at first, been a little overwhelmed and unsure of this generosity, but as time went on, it became a much-anticipated highlight in the week.

The doctor sighed. Times had changed. These young girls knew little about baking, or anything else for that matter. Now, any shop-bought treats were left on the coffee table upstairs. Dr Cosgrove rarely ventured upstairs to the staffroom unless caffeine was entirely necessary, but recently, she found she had let her guard down. Perhaps she was softening in her old age. Perhaps it was loneliness, but that morning, following Ruth's shocking statement, she couldn't bring herself to join them. Instead, she sat meditatively in her room until her first patient of mid-morning surgery arrived.

Dr Cosgrove called out the name, one she did not recognise. The practice was relatively quiet by this time with Ruth now attending to any house visit requests that had come in earlier. The elderly doctor squinted in the pool of sunlight that filtered from the skylight in the roof of the reception area. A pretty-looking woman who had been sitting on one of the low benches in the waiting room got up and approached her.

'Dr Cosgrove?' she asked, and extended a hand.

Dr Cosgrove was momentarily taken off guard. She didn't respond and left the woman standing with her hand outstretched. She stared for a moment or two, hardly able to comprehend. Her mouth was dry and her heart rate suddenly elevated. The sunlight from the waiting room was dazzling. The doctor involuntarily stepped back, her eyes flitting across the other woman's features. No. How could it be? What with the letters too, it seemed almost impossible. The memories came flooding back with such intensity that she was rendered breathless. Closing her mouth, Dr Cosgrove swallowed twice, her throat occluded completely. How, after all of these years?

The other woman had dropped her hand and was looking at her in concern. 'Dr Cosgrove? Are you all right?'

The doctor, whose eyes had been tightly shut, shook her head. She forced a smile. 'I'm so sorry.' She swallowed again and tried to compose herself. 'Yes. So sorry. I felt a little light-headed for a moment. I was miles away, I'm afraid.' She exhaled heavily. 'Miles away. You reminded me of someone I once knew. It was a long time ago. Long forgotten. You're a new patient though and not from these parts? I haven't seen you before? No, of course not. Excuse my rudeness, please come in. Sit down and tell me what I can do for you today.'

4

Looking up, Jean smiled. He hadn't changed so much after all. Long gone, though, were the boyish, fair curls, bleached with hours spent outdoors combing the clifftops or beating at overgrown umbellifers up and down the lanes. Instead, now, he was quite dark. His hair was cropped short and his forehead widened. But it was unmistakably him. Perhaps it was the half-smile that gave him away or the walk. Even at a young age he always had a conceit when he moved, as if he knew he was being admired. She watched him approach, casually raising a hand to the man behind the bar.

For a moment, she was unsure if he had seen her. She went to get up, pushing the chair back awkwardly and allowing the wood to scrape. But she had been wrong. She wondered if he had done it to tease, or perhaps he was playing it cool. It had been a long time after all and things were bound to have changed between them. Eventually, he allowed his gaze to fall on her and feeling slightly annoyed at herself, although she didn't know why, Jean stepped forward, her arms outstretched.

'So, you've come home at last,' she said. 'God knows why it's taken you ten years or more.'

'Jean.' He laughed and hugged her. His voice was deeper than she remembered and his body felt more angular. He pushed her away and looked down at her, his teeth slightly crooked and his left eyebrow raised. 'Jeanie Scott. All these years and you've not changed a bit.'

A corny line, but she liked it all the same. She knew she was blushing and suggested a drink. 'I'll get it,' she said, hoping he would argue and tell her to put her purse away, but when he didn't, and instead said he'd help her carry them over she felt a twinge of disappointment.

Twelve years it was. Twelve years. She had married, had a child, and divorced in that time, and he had been halfway around the world seeing things she couldn't even imagine. But he had returned.

It had all seemed so simple when they were fifteen and full of idealism. These days, Jean was jaded by the monotony of her maternal routine. She was stifled by the people of Kinnaven. There were no secrets here. Well, not for long anyway. But despite her irritation, her life seemed so impossibly entwined in the place that she knew it would be unbearable to leave. After Daniel had gone, she felt it might be her chance to get out also. She had searched for a job in the neighbouring town, even looked as far as the city. But something had stopped her. She pretended it was because she needed to stay close to her mother, who also lived in the village, but in truth, it was more than that. It was the place itself. Kinnaven held her there, trapped.

But this morning had been different. Gone was the drudgery of it all. She had woken early, and the sun streaming through the crack in her curtains seemed brighter and more energised than before. Going about her business that day, the people in the street who she had seen a thousand times before, smiled back at her, sharing in her optimism. Even the winding, cobbled streets she often cursed for tripping her, were more picturesque. As she turned at the top of the brae, breathless following her last job of the afternoon, she looked down on Kinnaven with new-found affection.

Ross was smiling at her now. The imperfect grin that he had always had. His canine teeth were slightly offset and she found herself transfixed. He had chosen a different table from the one she had laid her jacket beside. She had to nip back and collect it. The pub was quiet thankfully, but despite this, he had insisted they go to the very back. 'Just like old times.' He had laughed and again raised an eyebrow. Jean squirmed in recollection. Back then, the landlord had turned a blind eye to their underage drinking. Of course, he must have known. Even though Ross had been far taller than his peers, everyone knew everyone back then. It was the same when the minister had caught them in a fumbled embrace. Ross had been blasé, even proud to have been caught, but she had been mortified. The pub had changed hands twice since they were kids, but the minister was still the same. Jean saw him once a week and refused to meet his gaze, even now.

'Well,' she said. 'How does it feel to be back?'

Ross sipped his beer and sucked the line of foam from his upper lip, all the time making steady eye contact with her. She had forgotten how strange his eyes were. A pale blue with flecks of cobalt. Jean looked down at her hands and rubbed the now bare ring finger.

'Well, I've still to see Iain and Dad,' he said, finally looking away as a young couple entered the bar. Jean found herself following his gaze. 'The farm looks much the same,' he went on. 'More run down than when I was last here, I suppose. What are the locals making of my sister-in-law then?'

Jean rolled her eyes. 'You know I work for her, don't you?'

'I meant to say how ridiculous that is,' he said. 'What happened to your big plans? You were all set to go to

Aberdeen and study, weren't you? Didn't the hubby like that idea?'

Jean glanced up at him, hearing the scorn in his voice, but he was smiling and she wondered if she had imagined it. She supposed she deserved it. There had been an understanding of sorts when he joined up. A childish promise. But things had changed, and Ross had been as much to blame for that as her.

Initially, contact had been regular. That had been when he was in training. Telephone calls and letters. She had spent hours trying to compose something worthy to send him. She'd never been much of a writer. Neither had he. But when he had been sent abroad, it had all but stopped. She knew it was unfair to expect him to stay faithful. It had been a romantic notion. They had both been young. In reality, the whole thing was impossible. And then Daniel had arrived in Kinnaven, a breezy and attractive distraction. The telephone calls and letters had, of course, stopped completely after that. It was only following Daniel's departure, and eighteen months after their marriage had been negated, that she had dared to contact Ross again.

Despite being married, and with a child to another man, Jean had often found herself thinking of him over the years. He had returned briefly for his mother's funeral some nine months ago, but Jean had only heard of this after he had left. She had felt a deep pang of regret having missed her opportunity to see how he had turned out.

She had worried when he had first said he was joining the army. It had been a throwaway comment as they sat together on one of the huge concrete bunkers down on the clifftops. The man-made boulders had been placed there to stop enemy forces coming up and over the cliffs in the Second World War, so Jean's mum had said. Jean and Ross regularly sat there as children, gazing out to sea. Ross would lounge back on the stone and look up at her, and she would pick at the long grasses that crept up the edge, slitting them with her fingernails, and tucking her hair repeatedly behind her ear when it caught in the wind.

As they grew older, she would lie back also and look at the clouds as salty gusts wafted them past Ross's head. Sometimes, he would lean into her and kiss her face and mouth, pressing himself against her, and making her back ache. Then, she would close her eyes, wanting to heighten her senses, only opening them to find him laughing down at her. At those times, she would get annoyed and push him off, feeling she had been deceived in some way.

They had spoken about the army a good deal. Childish, fevered conversations about how they would maintain a relationship while he was away. She had been surprised at him wanting to leave Kinnaven, having assumed he would work the farm as his older brother now did. But when she thought about it, Ross had never shown any interest despite its likelihood to fall to him and his brother after his father died.

His brother, Iain, was a completely different person. He had always been first to offer help at harvest time or calving. Ross had been busy with other things. Iain had only returned to the village himself a short time before, having travelled to New Zealand, apparently working for an agricultural college. Jean had heard that he met his wife, Alison, out there. She was a fellow Scot who had moved briefly abroad to work also, but it seemed inevitable they might return to Iain's father's farm when the old man began to tire. The village had welcomed Iain back with open arms. Jean was unsure if it would feel the same way about his younger brother.

She knew Ross had been a disappointment to his parents. The countless disputes at school and complaints from the neighbours must have taken their toll. They had that in common, Jean thought years later when she considered what had led to their original relationship. She too had been a disappointment to her parents. Although it was not for the same reason, she most certainly felt it as strongly. That was why she had been so worried when he mentioned the army. Of course, for purely selfish reasons, she didn't want him to go, but there was something more. She knew that either following, or as a result of, his disharmony at home, Ross had a weakness of character. He was a lovable rogue and cheery, but he was easily led. Jean had heard stories of boys becoming thuggish after their time away. She did wonder how he might return.

'So, Jeanie Scott,' he said, cutting into her thoughts and making her smile. 'What have we got planned this evening now that husband of yours has buggered off out of here?'

Jean leaned back in her chair. It was as well she had arranged for her mum to take Calum that night. She'd not yet told Ross about her seven-year-old son and felt rather uncomfortable about doing so. But then, of course, Ross was bound to have matured during his time away. Perhaps he'd not mind so much about it.

'Well, I don't see any point in hanging around here,' Jean said, glancing towards the bar. 'Why not come over to mine for something to eat. You've plenty of time to see Iain and your dad. You've still to tell me about all of your adventures. You're skinnier than I expected. I suppose some of what you had to do and see was pretty awful?'

There was a pause while Ross took another draw from his pint. Jean watched the tawny liquid tip and touch his lips.

'Not really,' he replied, frowning. He placed the glass down on a cardboard coaster. 'Probably wasn't any worse than what I'd have had staying on here in this dump. I'll need to get a job soon though. I'm broke and I can't see myself working for Iain. I don't suppose anything is going? I'd take just about anything to get me started.'

She was a little surprised but tried not to show it. Perhaps he had seen some dreadful sights and wasn't yet able to talk about it. She had heard about post-traumatic stress disorder. In fact, she had only recently read up on it, anticipating such a thing. This might well be a sign. She was staggered to hear about the lack of funds though. She'd assumed he was well paid as a soldier.

'We'll treat ourselves, shall we, and get in a takeaway?' she asked, cheerfully. 'The next town delivers this far now, so we'd not need to go out. A curry maybe?'

'Well, you've come up in the world, Jean.' He laughed, having downed the last of his beer. 'I'd eat whatever's in the house, to be fair.'

Again, unease crept over her. How broke was he? This was certainly a new side to Ross. Growing up, he had always been more carefree and extravagant. Once, she had been horrified by how easily he could fritter away his money. There had been an air rifle. It had cost a good bit. She was sure he had only used the thing a handful of times to fire at the pigeons and gulls. Back then, it hadn't been his money, either. His father had paid both the brothers for doing odd jobs and helping around the farm, and being relatively well off, Jean assumed Ross had blagged extras on the side from his more indulgent mother. Since earning his own money for real, though, maybe he had begun to see its true value. Again, she let the matter drop and, having finished their drinks, they gathered their jackets.

Leaving the pub, they walked up Shore Road and onto Monduff Wynd. The late afternoon was warm, and the sky was now overcast. To Jean, it felt muggy and oppressive. Ross's stride was longer than hers and despite him slowing, she found it hard to keep in step. Linking an arm through his, she glanced up and saw him looking this way and that, taking in the memories of his childhood, all the old haunts. His expression was serious, and they spoke little as they made their way to the new houses near the top of the village. He had an air of melancholy about him. Maybe a few months back in Kinnaven, being fed and cared for, would bring him out of himself.

When they reached her house, he seemed to pull himself out of his mood and make more of an effort. She fumbled with the keys, her hands nervous and shaking, but he firmly took the bunch from her and while looking at her, slid the correct key perfectly into the lock, pushing the door with the toe of his shoe. Jean giggled. She knew as soon as they went in that her secret would be discovered. He didn't mention it but must have seen the child's jacket and shoes in the hallway. Instead of explaining, she led him through, hanging her jacket and handbag on the banister, and switching on the lights.

'I've not much to offer you,' she babbled, going through to the kitchen. 'Just pasta or frozen stuff, if you're sure you don't want to order in.'

He was behind her and turning, she hadn't realised how close he stood.

'I think you've got plenty to offer, Jeanie Scott,' he said.

When they made their way upstairs, she was self-conscious, realising her body was no longer that of the teenager he had once known. He seemed to sense her concern and having helped her undress, playfully traced the lines motherhood had bestowed on her. But when he kissed her, gone was the light-heartedness, and it was with a frightening intensity she had not known before.

As he lay in the bed beside her, his face now passive and relaxed in sleep, she felt increasingly anxious to talk with him more frankly. Still, she hadn't spoken of her marriage or Calum, and he had told her nothing of the last twelve years away from home. She wondered what his plans were. She was still to find out why he had decided to leave the army and return home in the first place. Had things reached their natural conclusion, and what would he now be qualified to do? At the back of her mind, she felt some unease. His reluctance to eat out and worse than that, his failure to pay for her drink in the pub were, of course, minor matters, but it did make her think something was wrong. Shouldn't the army have given out a lump sum when he was discharged? She was sure she had heard they did. If that was the case, where was the money? She supposed he would hook up with some friends he had met in the forces and find work that way but for the time being, she wasn't clear what had brought him back to Kinnaven. Although Jean was romantically minded, she didn't for a moment consider the draw to be herself. She wondered if it was something to do with the farm. There had been talk in the village about land being sold off. It had caused a bit of a stir. The last time she had been cleaning for the minister, he had been up in arms about the threat to the countryside and spoke about fields being sold for houses. Had Ross heard the rumour also? Jean wasn't sure how much contact he had had with his family while he was away. She supposed it wasn't up to him what his father did with the farm really, but if he was as strapped for cash as he said, he might have a vested interest, given the farm overall might go to him in the future. As she lay quietly beside him, she watched his chest rise and fall with each breath. His face was stubbled slightly and smiling, she rubbed her own chin, feeling the rawness he had left there.

When he finally woke, to her relief, he seemed more inclined to talk.

'So, where's the little boy then?' he asked as he stood by the window, his bottom half swathed in a towel and his chest bare. He had picked up a heart-shaped candle holder from the sill and turned it over in the palm of his hand.

'Come away from the window,' she hissed. 'The neighbours will see you and think I'm some kind of tart bringing men back from the pub.'

Ross turned and smiled. 'Well?' he asked.

'Calum's with my mum,' Jean said, getting out of bed herself and hastily covering up with a fleece dressing gown. 'He's seven. A bit of a troublemaker, and no interest in school, other than football, but he's a good boy. Mum often has him to help out and let me work.'

'You've still to explain that too.' Ross replaced the candle holder and moved on to her dresser. He picked up a couple of her earrings and let the gold hoops dangle on his finger. 'Well?' he asked, and although he grinned, she felt it was said with an accusatory tone.

'I was young and full of plans back then.' She sighed. 'I never would have stuck it at nursing college. I've no patience at all. And anyway, Calum came along and I took what I could get. I've got a good little list going and I work for myself.'

'Cleaning though?' he asked. 'You're better than that, Jean.'

'Well excuse me, but it's a job all the same, and one I'm damn good at. It's taken years to build up a set of regular clients and none of them complain. I pay my rent,' she said, and then, rather cruelly, 'and I can afford the odd takeaway for me and Calum when we fancy it too.'

She knew instantly that this was a step too far. She shot a glance across at him and instead of seeing anger, she was horrified to see his cocky attitude change to one of defeat.

'You're probably right,' he said quietly, replacing the earrings. 'I'd better get going and let you get on.'

She'd blown it.

'Ross...' she began, but he brushed past her and going through to the bathroom, quickly showered and dressed.

She busied herself downstairs putting the kettle on but knew he wouldn't stay. In the hallway, he kissed her on the cheek. 'Good to see you, Jeanie.' His voice was still flat.

'Ross, really, this is silly. If you're looking for work, I'm sure we can put our heads together and come up with something. I'll ask around, okay?'

He nodded and smiled, but she knew she hadn't fixed it. After he was gone, she found herself, for some reason, checking her bag that still hung on the stairs. Withdrawing her purse and unclipping the metal clasp, she saw that of the forty she knew should be there, now only ten remained.

5

As things turned out, Suzalinna was unable to travel with her. This caused her friend a good deal of concern and the whole trip was almost cancelled. But having already arranged the accommodation and with the blessing of Cathy's psychiatrist, it was agreed that Suzalinna would telephone every day and join Cathy as soon as was possible, once she had sorted out the 'bloody A&E department' and her 'useless' husband, poor, long-suffering Saj. Cathy knew Suzalinna was making light of her worries as she said this, and perhaps she could have delayed going, but now the idea of leaving town had been suggested, it was almost irresistible. Suzalinna had arranged the trip, but it had become Cathy's obsession. She had to get away. When Suzalinna said goodbye, she hugged Cathy for far longer than she usually would.

'I promise I'll be fine,' Cathy told her. 'Really, I will, and you know where I am.' She laughed at Suzalinna's frown. 'We'd be irritating the hell out of each other if you were coming with me. I need time on my own to think, Suz.'

Cathy set off just after seven. The sun was a mass of brilliant orange and the clouds touching its edges were barely feathers that wisped to nothing. She spent the car journey flicking between radio stations, following the local ones as she travelled north. Sometimes the advertisements became so drawn-out and painful that she switched to her CDs. She would rarely listen to a full track though, dismissing it, sometimes halfway through, often only after the first few chords. Had anyone travelled with her, they would have been maddened by her indecision. The journey took four hours in total. She was glad when she saw the signs for Aberdeen, knowing her destination would not be much further.

As she signalled right, pausing before leaving the trunk road and committing to Kinnaven village itself, she caught a glimpse of the shoreline from a different angle and shivered. The sea raged far below. Distant from the shore, two black columns of rock rose from the water, which whipped and spattered wave upon wave against them. Shaking off her apprehension, and putting it down to oversensitivity, Cathy turned towards the coast.

It was perhaps ten or fifteen years since she had last been this far north. The previous visit had been during their final year of medical school. The university had organised a small B&B as accommodation, not in Kinnaven itself, but a larger town along the coast, while they shadowed an overworked but enthusiastic consultant at the local district general.

It had been a happy time and essentially carefree. They were still unhindered by responsibility and could absorb themselves in ward rounds and teaching sessions without the distraction of accountability. As they were in their final year and deemed reasonably competent at least, they were entrusted with some of the minor day-to-day tasks that might prepare them for their year ahead as new junior doctors.

In many ways, their six-week stay had had a great impact on them both. Their mentor had seen Cathy's consulting style and had encouraged her to go in the direction of general practice. He had said something that touched her. She still remembered it. He could see a trait in her, a gentleness with the patients, a willingness to take more time than most would, and to him, that made her career a certainty.

Suzalinna was a different person altogether. She had knowledge and near-conceit that was obvious from the start. Whereas Cathy had been keen to listen to the elderly patients' stories on the ward, Suzalinna had been destined to deal with the sharper end of things. Whenever the crash bleep went off, signalling that a desperately ill patient needed immediate attention, her friend would drop everything and go. Despite not being on the team, Suzalinna would run, following the rest of the doctors, keen to be part of the action. It all seemed a lifetime ago now.

Cathy was so busy reminiscing that she almost missed the turn. The sign was weathered and worn, just as the buildings and sheds assigned to the place. As she pulled in at the gates, a dog barked and then the front door opened and a woman appeared. Her approach must have been watched for some time, as the track to the farm led to nowhere else, apparently.

Cathy judged that the woman was nearing the end of her third trimester. Her bump was neat and forward, her umbilicus jutting officiously through the fabric clinging to her. First-timer, Cathy guessed. Prims have an air about them that is unmistakable. The woman waved to direct Cathy around the edge of the yard, thus avoiding the mess, and once parked, she picked her way across, afraid of standing on something she should not.

'Hello?' the woman called, her voice catching on the wind, and Cathy saw how nice-looking she was. Her expression was pleasant and approachable, if not a little confused. Her face showed a puffiness around the eyes but was pretty. She was wearing a close-fitting T-shirt, leggings and fluffy slippers. Cathy found herself automatically scanning down and noting the swollen ankles. She wondered if the woman had had her blood pressure checked recently. Catching herself, she smiled. It wasn't her place to notice such things now, but it was a hard habit to drop when it had been her life for so long.

'Hi. I hope I'm in the right place? Kinnaven Farm Cottages? I'm Cathy.'

She offered her hand. The woman took it and said she was called Alison. The face remained friendly but puzzled.

'You found it all right then. Great.' There was an infinitesimal pause. 'Oh God. I'll admit it then,' Alison said. 'It'll be me. I'll be totally honest with you, Cathy, did you say? It was next week. Damn, I don't know what's wrong with me.' The woman stepped back and rubbed her forehead. 'Baby brain,' she said, 'and it's not even here yet. Next week is when I have you down, I think. Hang on a minute. You'd think I'd be able to... I hadn't been expecting anyone. This is bloody typical. I didn't used to be like this.'

Leaving her on the doorstep the woman ducked into the house and returned a few moments later with a spiral notepad. 'You'd never believe I used to be in charge of staff development and client liaisons back in the day, would you? Giving you a zero-star treatment now, amn't I?'

The attractive face frowned and her straight dark hair fell across her pale face as she leafed through the pages. 'Have you come a long way, then?' Alison asked, looking up and smiling. Her teeth were enviably even, and Cathy tasted a staleness on her own breath.

'Nearly four hours.' She was almost afraid to ask if they had a room for her after all. 'I've driven up from the Borders. I hope you've got something, I'm sorry to be a pest.' She knew she sounded desperate.

'No, it's not that. There's room. The house is empty. I've not had Jean in yet though. It wouldn't matter, but we've had berry-pickers all summer. Jean never stops telling me about the mess. I can't let you walk into that. She's not due until Tuesday because the schools are off.' Alison returned to her book, following the dates written down with her forefinger. 'Look, I have the twenty-second in here. Today's the fifteenth. I was sure I was right. I'm usually really good.' The woman looked up and smiled again, clearly pleased.

'I don't know what's happened then,' Cathy said, her stomach turning over. The thought of heading back out onto the road and looking elsewhere was not pleasant. She imagined herself trying to drive around, searching for a hotel or inn. She was completely drained of energy. If asked to go, Cathy thought she might well cry.

The other woman's face softened. 'Oh God, no, now I feel awful. You're exhausted from the drive and the place is empty. Don't leave us a bad review if it's a bit of a mess, okay?' she said. 'Don't panic. We'll get you sorted. I'll take you down there now. It's too late to worry about what went wrong with the booking. Let me put on some boots and I'll come down.' They both looked down at her slippers and Alison laughed. 'No, I'll not get far in these. I'll take the car and you can follow. Let me grab the keys. You'll have to excuse the mess if there is any. I'll try to get hold of Jean tomorrow if she's free. I hate not doing things properly. Jean'll give it a full check over, though. You're lucky it's empty, actually. We've been really busy.'

Cathy thanked the woman and after she had organised herself with the promised boots and keys, they both got into their cars with Alison signalling for her to follow in convoy. The Land Rover, which had been parked under a lean-to by one of the barns, turned rapidly in the yard ahead and with a crunching of loose dirt, accelerated onto the road, taking a sharp right. Cathy followed. The road soon twisted into a dirt track and she wished the woman would slow down, as the car's undercarriage was, at times, striking the odd stone or unexpected grassy bump. She struggled on and was relieved to see the Land Rover signal again. The car turned into a gap in the hedge that Cathy would have missed if she had driven alone. She followed tentatively and parked next to the other car, hoping not to hit a boulder, or God knows what else might have been there. The woman was out already and opening up the cottage. She began flicking on the lights as she moved through.

The cottage was small and had clearly been refurbished recently, but still retained enough of its original character to make it quaint. It seemed to be part of a long building. Cathy wondered if it had been extended in the past, or even split to make two semi-detached farm lets. Alison was making her way through the rooms, opening doors and checking to see if there was any of the predicted mess to clean. If she was anaemic, and Cathy had wondered given her pallor, she was without symptom and had more energy than Cathy herself. Cathy dropped her bag on the nearest chair and found the woman in the kitchen, already busying herself wiping surfaces.

'Please don't bother,' she said. 'I can do that myself. Just leave things as they are. I wasn't expecting anything fancy. It was our mistake anyway. The house is lovely. Just right. Please stop. It's fine as it is.'

'Give me five minutes,' Alison said, blowing a strand of hair from her face. 'I'll check the bathroom and make sure the sheets are okay. It's no bother. Jean usually does it so I'm not sure if she's replaced things. I need to check the cupboard here and then the bedding.'

Cathy stood awkwardly as the woman moved past her. She paused by the wall in front of her and shook her head, smiling. 'I always go to do that. There should be a door there really. It would make more sense.' She moved on to the bathroom and could be heard tutting. Cathy cringed. Deciding she was of no use standing watching, she returned to the car and pretended to be busy, getting her two overnight bags from the boot and locking it. The woman bustled back again as she re-entered the house, her arms, this time, full of sheets.

'I've stripped the bed in the back room and there are fresh sheets in the laundry cupboard. I'll send Jean to tidy things as soon as I can get hold of her. Oh, towels. Towels are in the cupboard.'

'Listen, I'm sorry about all this,' Cathy repeated. 'To have arrived like this.'

The woman was already moving through the front door, turning herself sideways to navigate her bump and the pile of sheets she carried before her.

'No bother, honestly,' she said. 'I hope it's just what you were after. Kinnaven's a bit quiet but it's not so bad. We've only been here for a full six months since we took over the farm properly from Iain's dad. Arthritis,' she said in explanation. 'Crippled with it, but fond of the odd drink still despite that.' Cathy smiled at this indiscretion. 'I felt at home right from the word go,' Alison went on. 'A lot of people say that when they come here. It's like they've been here before.' Cathy was going to explain that she had visited this area, albeit many years ago, but the woman was turning again towards the car. 'I'll get Jean in to do a proper tidy,' she called. 'Seriously, it's not usually as chaotic as this. Come up to the house if you need anything.'

'You must be due soon,' Cathy called out, almost as an after-thought, but Alison didn't hear and continued to the car.

Finally alone and, if truth be told, glad of it, Cathy stood in the garden looking out to sea. So, this was her home for the coming weeks. It could not be a greater contrast to the barred windows and magnolia walls of the hospital ward where she'd come from. She sighed and closed her eyes for a moment, feeling the salty breeze on her lips. The cottage was positioned well, perhaps far more thoughtfully than even the farmhouse which was set much further back. As far as Cathy could tell, Alison and her family had only a direct view of the coast from the left-hand side. Even this, she thought, might well be obscured by outbuildings.

She looked about her. The garden was barely that. Long grasses interweaved with red campion showed how far things had been allowed to slip, and the path leading to the front door was a crazy-paving of mismatched and uneven slabs. It was odd, Cathy thought, given how meticulous Alison seemed to be. She considered the pleasant woman, who in many ways seemed a paradox. Her admission to having previously worked in the corporate industry had not passed Cathy's attention, and yet how would anyone with such ambition and attention to detail end up here, in the middle of nowhere, contemplating a life dictated by the weather and seasons? Cathy supposed it was for the love of her husband, Iain, who she had mentioned; and where better to raise their child? Looking out to sea, she watched the endless dark water move like an animal frustrated by its confines, and for the second time that day, she felt an inexplicable sense of foreboding.

6

D r Cosgrove touched her forehead. Her hand trembled. The skin was cold and damp. Her breath came in short shudders. What was happening to her? She was right in the middle of her afternoon surgery too. Catching a glimpse of herself in the consulting room mirror, she saw her cheeks had become quite pale, her lips almost mauve. *Slow down*, she told herself, and she counted her breaths in and out. Three in, four out. Slowly, she told herself, just as she might instruct a patient. It took a matter of minutes and then she was able to see the colour returning to her face and to feel her fingers once more. She shook her head in disgust. What was all of this nonsense about? She was fine. She was in control and she was indeed a good person and an excellent doctor.

It was two weeks to the day since the first one had arrived. There had been more. Ridiculous. And with what purpose in mind? No matter how many nasty letters they sent, she was the one in the right. She was the doctor, after all. Dr Cosgrove nodded twice at her reflection. Indeed, she was. Had she not diagnosed an acute appendicitis that very morning and sent the young girl in for emergency assessment? She had quite possibly saved a life in doing so. She must tell Ruth about it for it was one of her regulars and in fact, the young girl had been in only the previous day to see their salaried GP with abdominal pain. Luckily for her, Dr Cosgrove had been astute enough to rescue the situation before it was too late. She must tell Ruth.

Her afternoon continued without event, but failing to catch up with her colleague that day, Dr Cosgrove left the surgery and made her short trip home. Arriving, the house felt empty and despite her desire for peace following the busy day, Dr Cosgrove stood in the hallway listening for a moment or two. No sound came, of course, other than the ticking of her grandfather clock, a much-loved heirloom passed down from her parents, and from theirs before them. Rousing herself, and seeing the cleaner had been, Dr Cosgrove smiled. A fine idea it had been. Just once a week, but it took a good deal of pressure off her. She was too tired after a long day at work to be bothering with dusting and vacuuming. But she was delaying, this she knew. She shook her head ruefully.

She walked through to the kitchen, picking up her post, which had been placed on the hall table by the cleaner. A quick bite and then she should get going. She had looked forward to the walk all day. The roads would be quiet and she longed to breathe the sea air and immerse herself fully in the late sunshine.

Putting it off no longer though, she began to leaf through the mail. It was all the usuals; she saw with relief. Two brown envelopes. Bills. For once, a blessing. One from the defence union, a circular. She got plenty of this type. And there was her journal. She had been waiting for it this last week and did enjoy the articles on general practice. Some were educational, others were quite witty. She smiled, recalling the previous month's satirical take on the new health minister's suggestions on tightening up spending in the community-based setting. Very droll. And that was it. The doctor smiled. She knew that it must finish at some point and they had become bored with the silly game. Dr Cosgrove shuffled the letters, stacking them in order of size. She was about to put the kettle on when she saw she had missed something. From beneath the journal, and stuck to the plastic sleeve covering this, she saw an edge of white. Her heart sank.

Lifting the *Journal of General Practice* between her fingers, she gingerly peeled the letter from it. The envelope was handwritten as the others had been and examining it, she saw it had the same postmark as the rest. She paused and took a deep breath. It was fine. She was in her own home and nobody could frighten her here. She was safe and in control. Carefully, she slid a finger under the lip and ran her fingernail across, making a perfect incision. The paper was cheap. A sheet of lined, white notepaper torn carelessly from a pad, the spiral entrails still drooping. It said: '1990' as she knew it must. Just that one year, written clearly and in bold lettering. The author had taken the trouble to go over the numbers at least twice and had pressed hard enough that the pen should almost come through at one point. She allowed the letter to drop and felt for the kitchen chair. Dr Cosgrove sat down unsteadily. *What now?*

She thought back to the summer of 1990. The darkest of her life. It was not long after her parents had died, some thirty years ago now. Her mother had gone first. Alzheimer's, such a cruel disease. Her father had passed only months later. On the certificate, they had said it was a myocardial infarction. She believed it was a broken heart. The thought sustained her to some degree. In life, her father had chaperoned her mother. It seemed only right that in death he might do the same. But oh, how she had grieved his choice to leave her to cope alone. She had walked the streets and countryside of Kinnaven, unseeing sometimes, guided only by the inner sense of sorrow. Dr

Cosgrove shook her head sadly. It had been before Ruth had come. Things might have been different had she been there. Perhaps with her to steady the ship, things might not have been so bad. It all might have been different.

During those dark days following her parents' death, she had operated as an automaton. Going through the motions, making all the right noises to her patients and doing her job the best she could. Looking back, she didn't know how she had managed, going in every day and listening to their trivial concerns, tending to their minor ailments. She had become a different person for a while. Embittered and sour. It had been out of self-preservation she supposed. A coping mechanism to propel her through those shadowy hours. All the while she had been somewhere else.

Although she had walked a great deal during those painful months, in her mind, she had walked far further. Her steps beat a rhythm over the Kinnaven countryside, trying to leave behind the hurt. Up past the church she would march, disturbing only the doves that roosted there, not seeing the acres of beauty surrounding her. Sometimes, she would find herself standing at the top of Whitmore Hill, the breeze blowing strands of her hair free from their pins. She had no purpose being there. She might stand for minutes or hours. Time had no meaning other than to signal her expected return to the practice.

During that time, her parents had felt oppressively close. Sometimes, she guiltily longed for some space, to be alone and free of their attention. She wondered if she was trying to escape not only the grief but their presence also. But this thought had made her indescribably sad.

Dr Cosgrove left the kitchen and, carrying the letter with her, she crossed to the fireplace in the front room. She bent slowly. Her back ached these days, along with her hips and knees. The fire was laid already. It only needed a match. The kindling was dry and would take quickly. This one would go the same way as the others. She had not invited such intrusion into her house. She would not be frightened or bullied by anyone. The click came as she struck the matchstick against the box, then the flame, which she shielded with her hand, leaning forward and allowing it to touch the paper. It caught at the corner, singeing a dark line along the edge until it finally took hold and the letter was consumed. Breathlessly, the old doctor straightened. On the mantelpiece, a photograph of her parents looked down.

She sat down in her armchair, as the fire burned itself out. The old doctor allowed her breathing to return to its normal rhythm. In and out. That was right.

She felt him before she saw him and the relief was immense.

'Father, what should I do?' she asked. 'I'm afraid.'

Her father nodded wisely but didn't answer. Her mother was in the distance, dancing alone in her fur coat and high heels.

7

Jean had been going to Mrs Spratt's for almost five years now. It was a small, mid-terraced house. Nothing fancy. White exterior walls and the mobility handrail by the door gave away its resident's age. Mrs Spratt had lived alone for as long as Jean could remember. Her mother had told her she had lost her husband and son in the war, but Jean had never asked and Mrs Spratt hadn't offered the information.

She found it simple from a cleaning point of view, even though her responsibilities had increased over the years as Mrs Spratt's capabilities had lessened. But that morning, despite her affection for the old lady, Jean found her thoughts wandering as she listened to her talk.

'What was that, Mrs Spratt?' she repeated.

'The farm,' Mrs Spratt said. 'I know you clean up there. I'd wondered if you'd heard. The minister's organising some sort of a meeting. Mrs Hutchison popped her head in earlier to say, asking if I'd be fit to attend. Of course, I said no. I'll need to get Dr Cosgrove in again, although it pains me to do so.'

Jean paused, her duster hovering mid-air. 'You're talking about the development? Is that what you mean?'

'Yes, the development. Haven't you heard a thing I've said?' Mrs Spratt's voice was heavy with exasperation. 'They're all up in arms over it. I don't suppose it'll make the slightest bit of difference stirring up ill-feeling. It's the old devil's land and if he's set his heart on selling it off, that's his business.'

Jean smiled down at the elderly lady who sat in her chosen armchair by the electric fire. She was a small woman, perhaps shrunken with age. Her face had rather an acetic quality, with fragile pale skin sagging to a pointed chin.

'I've not heard a thing,' she said, truthfully. 'I know the youngest son's back though, so that might cause a bit of a stir.'

Mrs Spratt shot her a look. Jean blushed, knowing she had failed to hide the pleasure in her voice.

'That hooligan?' the old lady asked. 'The second boy who joined the army? He was a friend of yours, I seem to remember. Watch yourself with that one if he comes sniffing around, Jean Scott.'

Jean couldn't help but smile at her turn of phrase.

'I know the army can change a man, but in his case, it would have had to be a complete transformation.'

Mrs Spratt looked up once more and Jean nodded. 'Well?' Mrs Spratt said, but Jean didn't answer and continued to dust.

He had, in fact, left it until the previous evening to return, a full forty-eight hours since she had seen him last. Having spent the entire day questioning herself over the missing money from her purse, Jean still felt horribly worried. But when he arrived at her door, a bottle of wine in one hand and a garish box containing a water pistol for Calum, she let him in, hating herself for considering an ulterior motive. The boys became acquainted easily, and Jean felt even further ashamed as she watched Ross kneeling on the living room floor beside her son, grappling to remove the packaging from the gun, so it could be deployed immediately. Before long, she had all but convinced herself of her mistake. The money had been a mix-up, she had lost it, or had spent it without thinking. How could she have thought it stolen, and by Ross of all people? Sitting on the arm of the sofa, she nodded as Calum, brandishing his new weapon, raced through to the bathroom to fill it with water from the sink.

'Outside,' she called through and then turning to Ross, she rolled her eyes. 'I wasn't so sure you'd be back after you left in a temper,' she said, looking down as he collected the scraps of cardboard and cellophane from the floor. She expected him to say sorry, that he was always going to return. They were old friends, after all, and far more than that. But instead, he continued to tidy and for a moment or two, she wondered if he had heard her at all.

'You've changed, Jean,' he said, shaking his head. And finally, looking up, Jean saw the intense cobalt blue and wondered what he meant. A wave of indignation welled up in her and she fought to stop herself from asking him just what the hell he was talking about. He was the one who had changed. These sulky black moods were entirely new. Before he had gone, they had argued, naturally. They had been children essentially, after all, but both had been quick to repent. Since his return, Jean had seen it several times, a new side to Ross, a petulant, moroseness she hadn't known before. So quick to take offence, so changeable. He had returned to Kinnaven of his own free will. She'd not gone begging for his company. His manner had been odd, to say the least, swinging from playfulness to deepest misery. She felt inclined to ask some pretty searching questions, but at that moment, Calum ran back through, dripping water all over the carpet.

Shaking off his pessimism, Ross chased the boy through the kitchen and out the back of the house to the small yard behind. Jean followed them slowly, listening to Calum's excited squeals and Ross's taunts and laughter. She couldn't understand his behaviour at all.

It wasn't until far later that evening they had a chance to talk. Calum, exhausted by his new and boisterous playmate, had collapsed wearily in bed, his new prized possession, after much argument, left in the bath rather than being placed on top of the duvet.

When she came downstairs, Ross had already opened the wine and poured two glasses. 'Peace offering,' he stated and she paused and smiled, her hand still on the banister.

'I hate it when we fall out,' she said, 'and you're hardly home a day or two as well.' She took the glass and raised it. 'What should we drink to, then?'

'To new beginnings, of course, and happier times for both of us,' he said.

The alcohol freed Ross, and sipping her own slowly, as she usually stuck to heavily-diluted vodka and tonic, Jean watched the tension leave him. He relaxed back in the armchair and grew drowsier. His eyes lost their sharp intensity that had startled her before. They initially talked generalities, but soon, seeing him more relaxed, she felt able to broach the matter of his unexplained circumstances.

'Have you spoken to Iain yet about a job?' she began. 'I know you said you needed something soon, but you'll take some time to readjust to civilian life. It must have been a strain. It'll be quite a change now, coming away from all that routine and discipline.'

Ross leaned forward and placed his glass down on the carpet, holding the edge as he waited to see if the fibres beneath would tip the liquid over. 'I've not spoken about work, if I'm honest, Jean.' He sighed and, now content that his drink wasn't going to spill, he extended his arms up, stretching them over his head, and groaned. 'Iain's caught up with the baby being due.

Alison's nipping at him at every opportunity and she's unimpressed to have yours truly turning up expecting bed and board.'

'What about your dad?' she asked, taking another sip, inwardly grimacing at the taste.

'The old bugger hasn't changed a bit, has he?' Ross retrieved his glass from the floor and took a swig. 'Troubled with his joints but more than capable of unscrewing the whisky bottle and doling out orders. God knows how Iain can stick it.'

'I suppose he's used to it. What is it they say about farmers never retiring? It's hardly a surprise that your dad would struggle to let the place go.'

Ross shook his head. 'I couldn't do it. Couldn't stand living up there day after day. Even after the old man carks it, I'll not be tempted.' Ross turned and looked at Jean. 'What do you make of her then? Alison, I mean? What do you think?'

'She's been nice enough to me. I go in and do the big house once a week and there are the holiday lets she's started up too. I'm glad of the extra work. The only odd bit is your dad's place. That's completely off limits. He's been out of the farmhouse and in the workers' cottage a good six months now, and I've never set foot in it. Not been asked to. I suppose it suits him better being on one level now without stairs to climb up and down. I assume Alison keeps an eye on things or your brother, but you'd have thought they'd need me in there to give things a bit of a clean from time to time. Anyway,' Jean looked across at Ross, 'what are you going to do then? I'd assumed you'd meet up with some of the other lads from the army if you weren't wanting to work on the farm. Perhaps something's going in Aberdeen. Have you been discharged with any special training?'

Ross snorted but said nothing.

'I just thought...' Jean began, but didn't know what to say. She looked across at him and saw again the unhappiness. At that moment, her frustration and confusion dissolved, and she felt only an overwhelming pity. She saw the young boy from all of those years ago, but far more lost and confused than he had ever been before. He was right in what he'd said earlier. She was the one who had changed, and perhaps not for the better. She had failed to see how hopeless and depressed he was. Perhaps jaded by her failed marriage, she had been suspicious of his motives and had assumed the worst. A crushing desire to help him obliterated all her previous misconceptions. She went to him and crouched down by his chair. She touched his knee and looked into his face. She no longer saw the eyes of a man, but those of a frightened boy.

'Ross, you need to tell me,' she said, unable to hide her emotion.

He looked away.

'You must tell me. I don't know what's happened before, but you know I'll do all I can to help. If you'd rather stay here for a while until you get yourself sorted...'

But he was shaking his head. 'It's not that. It's not the farm. Oh God, Jean, I don't know where to start. Things are out of my control.' He raised a hand and rubbed it across his face, shielding his eyes from her. 'Oh God, Jean. It's pretty bad.'

She held him to her and rocked him almost as she had done with Calum as a toddler, even now, she still did if he came running home crying with scraped knees. 'It'll work out fine,' she soothed, breathing into his cropped hair, 'but you need to tell me what's wrong.' She sensed a change in him and drew back. He was steeling himself.

'I'll tell you then, but you won't like it.' He leaned back and sighed. 'I never meant to bring my troubles to your door, Jean, really I didn't, but you're the only one now. The only person I can trust.'

She nodded but didn't speak, so he began.

'In the army, you have to spend money to get on with folk,' he said.

Jean rocked back on her heels and settled herself at his feet properly to listen.

'I suppose I've always been a bit of an idiot with money, you know that,' he said. 'The problem was when I ran out of wages earlier than the end of the month and had nothing left to go on. I had to scrabble around a bit. It's not as if I stole,' he said defensively, perhaps sensing her apprehension, 'but I did borrow, and take out loans.' He paused and waited for her to speak, but when she said nothing, he continued, 'Well, you can imagine how that ended. The debts were getting bigger and bigger and people were getting angry. It came to a head at the end of last year when I thought I'd come up with the answer.' He shot Jean a look and she saw again the frightened eyes. 'I came up with a bit of a plan, as it happens, of selling on cheap tobacco to some of the lads. That's what started it, but, of course, they could get their own and at almost the same price as the poorer quality gear I was bringing. So, then I thought about other stuff.'

Jean, now knowing exactly where this was headed, looked down at her hands.

'It wasn't anything serious, Jeanie, just a bit of weed for heaven's sake, but you can imagine how strict the army would have been if they found out.'

'And did they?' she asked, now feeling numb. 'Is that why you're home then? Because you've been kicked out?'

'No,' he almost shouted, and Jean raised a hand to quieten him. He continued, spitting his words at her in a whisper. 'No, I wasn't kicked out. How could you say that? They didn't suspect a thing. A few of the lads who regularly bought from me got a bit agitated about it all though and I thought it best to bow out gracefully.'

'They were going to blackmail you?'

'In a way.' He nodded. 'Leaving, anyway, was the best bet, and I was done with the whole thing. You can only take so much of that, Jean. The sights you see and the things they ask you to do. The number of nights I've lain awake reliving the horrors, and when I have slept, crying out and waking in a cold sweat.'

'Poor Ross,' she murmured. 'I'm so sorry it's ended this way for you. I understand,' she went on, feeling he needed further reassurance. 'Really, I can see you weren't in a sound state of mind. It's called post-traumatic stress disorder and I'm sure that if the army ever had found out about the drugs, they would have discharged you but you'd have been exonerated of any blame.'

Ross seemed surprised and a little overwhelmed. She thought he was going to kiss her, but he looked away once more. 'You're too good to me, Jeanie,' he said. 'Far too good.'

'If money is worrying you, then I have a little put by after the divorce settlement. Daniel's moved on and now works on the rigs, so he's taking care of Calum for the most part. That leaves my earnings for utilities and savings. We'll get by,' she said. 'I'm glad you told me. I knew something was wrong.'

'I'd pay you back, of course,' Ross said, clearing his throat. 'I can't believe it's happened. How can I ask you to support me when it should be the other way around?'

Jean ignored his words. 'In the meantime,' she said cheerfully, 'and I hope you don't mind me suggesting it, but I did have a thought about your situation this last day, actually. If you're sure you're not keen on the farm?' Jean paused. 'Clearly not,' she said, seeing his pained expression. Now relieved to be more light-hearted, she continued, 'So obviously, it's just a stop-gap until something better comes along, but they're looking for help at the surgery. I clean for the doctor twice a week. I even do her house in the village. I had heard some mention of them needing a bit of simple joinery work done at the practice. Just shelves putting up and that sort of thing. Perhaps mirrors hung and a few odd bits and bobs. I know it's not much, but it might lead to something more, you never know.'

'I think, Jeanie Scott, you are a very beautiful and wonderful woman,' he said seriously. He removed the glass of wine from her hand and placed it deliberately and slowly down on the ground. 'And,' he continued, his eyes now locked on hers, 'I would like to show my gratitude to you right here and now.'

~

Jean grinned, unable to help herself.

'Well, then?' Mrs Spratt said, interrupting her from further rumination on her lustful nocturnal escapades. Jean wondered how long the old woman had been watching her.

'Sorry, Mrs Spratt,' she said. 'I was miles away.'

'Well, you heed my warning about that young army lad,' the old lady said.

Jean smiled. It was so like the old woman to be judgemental. Just like the rest of Kinnaven. Stuck in the past and unable to move forward. Jean felt sure she had misjudged poor Ross and was steadfast in her resolve to save him from further upset. But as the days passed, allowing her and Ross to become more deeply involved, certain incidents reawakened her fears. Still, though, she could not have foreseen the tragedy that lay ahead. Perhaps it was just as well.

8

Having finished at Mrs Spratt's house that morning and promising the old lady she would listen out for any further news about the land being sold, Jean set off through the village to the GP's surgery. She didn't usually clean for the doctors on a Tuesday and a couple of the receptionists raised their eyebrows when she walked in.

'Is she free?' she asked Frances, one of the girls who worked behind the desk.

'Who? Dr Cosgrove? She is, as it happens. In a bit of a temper when I took a pile of scrips for her to sign.'

Jean, although dreading the interaction now, knew that she must do it, and the sooner the better before she lost her nerve. She crossed the waiting room and tapped gently at the doctor's consulting room door. It was perhaps half a minute before the door opened.

'Yes? Can I help you?' the doctor asked, obviously not recognising the girl who cleaned for her.

'I'm sorry to bother you when you're sure to be very busy, Dr Cosgrove. I'm the cleaner, Jean. I wondered if I might have a word?' Jean swallowed and clasped her hands to stop them shaking.

The doctor, clearly not used to such a liberty, looked up and down the corridor as if searching for an alternative, but seeing none, nodded quickly and stepped aside allowing her to enter. 'I'm afraid it will have to be brief,' the doctor began. 'If it's something medical, I will need to ask you to make an appointment.'

'Oh no, it's nothing like that,' Jean reassured her. 'I'd heard you needed some odd jobs done about the practice. One of the receptionists mentioned it the other week.'

Jean wasn't sure what happened to her that day. In fact, she wasn't sure quite what she said but she managed the discussion with some tact, and following their five-minute conversation, Dr Cosgrove was persuaded that the young army boy would suit her purpose very well indeed. When she saw Jean to the door, it was with a different attitude to before. She even thanked the cleaner for her recommendation, adding that if she was correct in her thinking, then perhaps a regular maintenance man might be of some use to the practice after all. Providing this Ross fellow worked out, she would consider making it more permanent.

Jean was in no doubt whatsoever that Ross would meet Dr Cosgrove's expectations and more. Inwardly she hugged herself and hoped the opportunity would boost Ross's morale and perhaps lead to bigger and better things.

Ross did not fail her. Following his first week on the job, it was clear to all at the practice that his quiet, sociable manner and skilled and able joinery would indeed be an asset. Jean knew it was only a matter of time before the doctor, who she considered more pliable than she made out, would fall for his charms and make the position permanent.

Jean and Ross had now settled into something of a routine.

Still, though, Jean felt a sense of unease. She was certain something was troubling him. Sometimes, when they sat together watching the television flicker against the darkening walls of her room, Jean would glance sideways and see a look of concern. More and more, when he thought that he was unobserved, she was convinced his cobalt eyes were filled with fear.

She asked him a couple of times if there was something on his mind, but smiling at her, he would dismiss the suggestion, rallying himself and becoming cheerful once again. Jean felt helpless and, on the odd occasion, angry that he wouldn't take her into his confidence. She supposed, however, that it was caused by his reflections on the past horrors seen in the army and, having read a good deal on the matter in women's magazines, she wondered if it was best not to dig too deep.

She discussed the situation with her mother, who although delighted to see her only child now happy at last, was troubled.

'Don't go opening up old wounds,' her mother advised, as they sat together in the kitchen sipping tea and putting the world to rights. Jean nodded in agreement. Of course, her mum was quite correct. Best not to pry.

It was a fortnight after starting his work at the doctors' practice when Jean first became aware of a problem. Calum was over at a friend's house for the night and it was just the two of them for the evening. She had planned a special meal and had even been to the next town to buy something nice for pudding. She would have a shower and wash her hair before Ross arrived.

By this time, Ross had all but officially moved in with her and Calum. Many nights he didn't bother to return to the farm, saying he felt more relaxed in her company anyway, as Iain and Alison were preoccupied with their own affairs. Jean's heart had swelled when he said this and she had hesitantly suggested that he leave a few things at her place, a toothbrush and change of clothes at the very least, to save him returning to the farmhouse first thing in the morning before going into work. She had even shown him where the spare key was kept, under a rock near the front door, and had encouraged him to use it when needed.

That afternoon, Jean came home to find the door unlocked and Ross's shoes lying by the porch. Knowing that he must be back early she called out as she went into the house.

'Ross? Is that you?' She slipped her handbag from her shoulder and hanging it, as she always did, along with her jacket on the banister. The shopping bags, she laid on the floor by the door, her hands indented from their weight having carried them in from the car.

When she saw him, she knew immediately that something was different. He came through from the kitchen, his steps falling with a jauntiness she had not seen in some time. On his face was an uneven and infectious smile. He lifted her and swung her around the small hallway. Jean banged her ankle on the table that housed her keys and the telephone and cried out for him to put her down and stop fooling about. He allowed her to slide down and then, taking her face in his hands, leaned down and kissed her forcibly on the lips, without saying a word.

'What on earth?' she finally said, stepping back. She was, of course, delighted to find him in such high spirits, but why she couldn't imagine. In his eyes now was an excitement of near manic proportion. Taking her hand, he led her through to the kitchen where he had already boiled the kettle in readiness for her return.

'We're going out, Jeanie,' he announced. 'I'm taking you and we're eating out. Our fortunes have finally changed.'

She laughed. 'What on earth's happened? Have you won the lottery then?'

He snorted. 'No luck needed, Jean, just patience and I have plenty of that. You know, I really feel for the first time since

coming back to this place, that I might just make a go of things.'
He looked down at her. 'And that means with you, Jean. This is
the sign I've been waiting for. I know with you by my side, I'm
going to be fine. Without your help these past few weeks, I
might have given the whole thing up. You, me, and little Calum
are going to get out of this place and on to better things.'

'But I still don't understand,' she said, shaking her head as
she poured boiling water from the kettle into two mugs. 'What
exactly has changed.'

'I finished working up at the surgery early this morning.
They only had a few things that needed doing and it's all so easy,
really. The old doctor doesn't have a clue how simple some of
the jobs she asks me to do are. Anyway, I went up to the farm
before I came back here and I spoke to Dad. It seems he and Iain
have had a bit of a falling out. Sounds like the golden boy isn't so
great all of a sudden and Dad, well, for the first time, Jean, he
told me he was proud of me. Said he could see I was trying to
make a go of things since coming out of the army.'

Jean put Ross's mug down in front of him. 'Oh, Ross,' she
said. 'Of course, he's proud.'

Ross rolled his eyes. 'He's never shown it in the past, has he?
It's only been worse since Mum died last year. Anyway, it sounds
like Dad's finally winding down. He mentioned the developers
again, and apparently they're pushing for moving ahead with
planning, if he really is willing to sell.'

'And is he? I thought it was still a cause for concern, splitting
the farm,' she said, sipping at her tea. The matter had been
mentioned several times over the past few weeks and Jean had
all but convinced herself that at the end of the day, the old
farmer wouldn't bring himself to do it. 'They might not get
permission to build houses anyway,' she went on. 'Half of the
village is protesting already. You should have heard the minister
when I was up there the other week.'

Ross grunted. 'You've no idea. These big developers get what they want. Of course, it'll get objections from the locals. They expect that. But they'll get their way, and if they do, just think of the money.'

'But it wouldn't be yours. It would be your father who would profit,' she said defiantly, but she, of course, knew what he meant. Ross's father was hardly in the best of health and they had even openly discussed what might happen if he died, leaving the farm to Iain at worst, or possibly, if he played fair, splitting the estate between the two brothers. In the past, though, Ross had gloomily told her that his father would be unlikely to split it, given his disinterest in the business over the years, and Iain and Alison might get everything. Things had, after all, been difficult when Ross had left Kinnaven originally. At the time, his father had openly announced that Ross should expect nothing of his inheritance and back then, Ross could not have cared less. Since then, though, things had changed.

'I want us to get married, Jean,' Ross said impulsively, and to her look of astonishment, he continued, 'Not now, of course, but in the future. Imagine what kind of life we would have with money in our pockets. Just think how different it could all be for Calum too.'

It was very hard for even sensible Jean to think logically after that. He had offered her what she had always dreamt of: a life together, free from worry over when the next bill might be paid, or having to save for some school trip for Calum. More importantly, since his return, she had become increasingly convinced they were destined to be together once more. They had both taken time apart to grow up. Both had made mistakes along the way, but once reunited, they had been firm in their affection.

Jean looked up at him with a new-found admiration and love. He was going to make their little family official. Perhaps not immediately, but they would marry, and even go on to have more children. Jean considered this and thought of Calum's future also. How wonderful for him to have someone stable and reliable in his life once more. A real male role-model to look up to, now his father had gone.

'Well, I suppose we should celebrate,' she said. 'But you know I'm done this month after paying for Calum's new shoes.' Although things were fine, she could hardly say she was doing well, and already, Ross had borrowed a little of her savings to buy a few necessary tools for the work up at the surgery.

Ross reached into his trouser pocket and pulling out a wad of ten-pound notes, dropped them carelessly on the kitchen counter.

'Did the doctor give you an advance or something?' she asked. When he didn't answer, she shot him a look. 'Ross?' she said, now concerned. 'Where's the money come from?'

He turned and made to come towards her. But knowing he was going to try to kiss her again, she turned away. 'Ross?' she repeated.

'Sweetheart,' he began and she knew it was trouble because he never called her that. 'Darling, it's borrowed and that's the truth of it. You know I can't lie to you because I love you so much. You and little Calum. It's borrowed and I'll return it as soon as Dad sells up. Why should we live like paupers when we know what's coming our way so soon?'

'Borrowed?' she repeated, suddenly feeling cold. 'Borrowed? I thought you weren't going to get into more debt again. You promised we'd talk if you needed money for anything.'

'I don't mean that. I've not taken a loan,' Ross said.

'Then what? Has your father lent it to you? Tell me, Ross, you're scaring me. You've been in Kinnaven all day and only at the farm and the doctors... Oh God, Ross, tell me you haven't.'

Jean felt as if she was in the grip of a nightmare. Surely, he couldn't have taken the money from someone at work.

'No, no, Jean, listen. It's not like that at all. It's not the doctor's personal money, don't be ridiculous. What do you think I am?'

Jean's hands were trembling now and she steadied herself against the kitchen worktop. He made a couple of attempts to start, and when he did, she could only listen in horror and wait for it to end.

He had been putting up pigeon holes behind the front reception desk. The office girls and he had been having a bit of a carry-on in between the patients coming for their appointments. One bad-tempered man had come to the desk and given the girls a bit of a dressing down. He said the man was throwing his weight around over some insurance claim he had asked the doctors to fill out, or a letter they had to write, or some such nonsense. Anyway, the girls, when they explained there would be a charge, received nothing but abuse from the man. Quite arrogant and nasty he was, but the receptionists had told him without the fee he wasn't getting the letter, and that was how it was with everyone.

Well, Ross had found himself stepping in and he told the man to stop giving the girls a hard time and it was only them doing their job. After a good bit of huffing and puffing, the man had pulled out his wallet and paid. Fifty pounds it had been. The girls had handed over the letter and that was that.

Ross had asked them if it was par for the course, getting spoken to in that way, and they said it happened all the time, especially when there was a charge involved. Ross told them they deserved a medal to put up with it, and the receptionists said they would prefer better pay really, but the old doctor was a bit tight. They had all laughed a good deal over that. Ross had then told them he rarely saw the old doctor, and when he did, she was busy, but the girls said she was a right horror to work for sometimes and many of the patients found her harsh too.

Ross told Jean he had continued to fix the shelving for another hour or so and when the girls went upstairs for coffee. Leaving him to it, he had seen the deposit box and something in him had made him think.

'It was an accident,' he said. 'A moment of madness, but the more I thought about it, the more sense it made. I opened the box and took the fifty quid. There was more in there too. Another hundred. I took it too. Then it was too late to put it back. One of the girls came through and I was stuck. It was for us,' he said, looking at her with his piercing blue eyes. 'I did it for us, Jeanie. Just until my dad comes good with the money from the farm. Why should we go on living hand to mouth when people like that snobby doctor don't even realise the money's sitting there? A hundred and fifty quid's nothing to them, but it makes all the difference to us. Jean, don't look like that. I told you I love you and I only did it because I know I'll get money from the farm.'

Turning from him, she covered her face with her hands and sobbed as if her heart was breaking. In that final sentence, she knew he had lied.

9

Cathy had set herself a deadline of three months. If she was no better within that time, she would relinquish the partnership. It was the only fair thing to do. She couldn't expect her colleagues to wait around, filling her sessions with inadequate locums. She set her jaw. She had fought to get the job in the first place, but she wasn't going to be a burden. Not to her colleagues who she respected, but more importantly, not to her patients. Their care came above her pride. James and Mark would find a replacement. Another female partner to balance the dynamic, perhaps? Cathy swallowed, but her throat ached with the lump lodged there. She remembered how thrilled she had been to get the job originally. How she and Suzalinna had celebrated together on hearing the news, dancing around her friend's kitchen table, Cathy's eyes shining with relief, and her friend smiling in amusement.

'Finally!' Cathy had whooped again and again. 'Finally, I've got there. I thought getting the exams was the hardest part, but this, finally landing a partnership, this is it! I've made it!'

'Darling, it's not been that long,' her friend had laughed. 'It was only the third interview.'

But perhaps Suzalinna didn't understand. They'd never spoken about it. With each polite rejection following an interview, a part of Cathy had wilted. They could see her for what she was. She had the same qualifications as the rest of the candidates, but they must recognise the anxiety in her eyes. It was called 'imposter syndrome'. The fear of being exposed as a fraud. Had she deserved to make it through medical school and her house jobs at all? Had it been chance that no one had found out she was winging it?

Over the years, Cathy had watched Suzalinna in guilt-ridden envy as she collected her college exams without falter. Of course, Suzalinna had studied. Many times, Cathy had phoned for a chat during the evening, only to be told by Saj she had left instructions that she was not to be disturbed. Still though, in some ways, it did seem that things had fallen at Suzalinna's feet. 'Born lucky' her friend had jokingly said when she had been shortlisted for an accident and emergency consultant post at her preferred hospital. Cathy appreciated that it was more than luck. Suzalinna had worked hard, and her steely determination had got her where she deserved to be. But how Cathy had wished things had come to her with as much ease.

It made it all the more agonising to have it ripped from her grasp. Her calling, her vocation. General practice was what she had been destined to do. *Funny though*, she thought, *it does feel as if I'm watching rather than participating in life at the moment.* Since she had arrived in Kinnaven four days ago, time had stood still. She felt powerless to make herself well again. They had all made it clear that she should take as long as necessary but she wasn't a fool and knew no partnership could last the indefinite absence of one of its team.

'What can I do?' she had asked her psychiatrist, twisting her hands in her lap during her final session before leaving the hospital. 'I'll do anything. Hypnosis, CBT, counselling. Whatever it takes to get back to work.'

He had smiled slightly. After several weeks of inpatient treatment, they had become better acquainted and her desperation probably came as less of a shock as it might have first done. Cathy knew that she sounded pathetic. It was like bargaining with God during the stages of grief, except in her circumstances, she was bargaining with her psychiatrist to keep her sanity and vocation.

He had advised that the less she 'tried' perhaps, the better. 'Take the tablets and rest,' he recommended. 'I can't make promises. It's your first presentation. You're young and you have a good reason to get well. I hope you will do so, but I can't make guarantees.'

And so, Cathy found herself without purpose, perhaps for the first time in her life. There had always been a goal, an exam to pass, a job to succeed at, a patient to save. Now, she was at the mercy of time. She prayed that her mind would heal itself and, at least for the initial few days, she tried to relax into Kinnaven's slower pace of life.

Although Cathy was not one of the long-term inhabitants, she felt the longer she stayed there, the more bound she became to the hamlet. She had taken her pills as prescribed by her psychiatrist, she had breathed in the sea air and exercised as instructed by her overzealous friend, Suzalinna. They had spoken a couple of times on the phone. Initially, Cathy had chastised her friend for the booking error, but telephone reception was poor and feeling perhaps more emotionally distant from her, Cathy had several times ignored her calls, feeling unable to respond in the way she knew Suzalinna might want. Looking out to sea, she wished herself well again. But if the days dragged by, it was the nights that had been the real problem. She supposed her mind must be its most active then.

When she did manage to sleep, her dreams were filled with nightmarish images and thoughts.

The previous night, she had dreamt she was falling. She fell hard and fast towards rocks far below. The height must have been considerable because she was mid-air for what seemed like an eternity, watching the waves race towards her. As she landed, she heard laughter, crazed and irrational. Perhaps it was her own. It was the final sound before her face smashed and splintered on the shingle. That was when she woke. It had been the same so many times over. Jolted into consciousness.

That morning, still woozy from her bad night, she sat outside in the sun. The cottage, although neat and picturesque, was undoubtedly cold. She had been surprised at this, finding often that sitting on the doorstep was a good deal more comfortable than residing in the house itself some mornings.

It was in this position, following breakfast that day, her head rested languidly back against the cool stone of the building and her legs outstretched on the mossy ground, that she was first aware of being watched. Although her own eyes were closed to the glare of the sun, she knew it immediately. Before her, the sea raged and pummelled on the rocks below. Cathy shifted her weight and, shading her eyes, looked behind and to the left of her, up onto the moorland which surrounded the cottage. As far as she knew, it was only reached by the road belonging to the farm and unless someone had walked past before she had come outside, she wasn't sure how they had got there. The figure above her moved uncertainly, perhaps aware they were being watched. Cathy strained her eyes to make out who it was. She thought she could see a hat but due to the angle of the sun, she could only really identify a shadowy outline. She believed it was a man, or rather, she had a feeling it was. She sat perfectly still, watching herself being watched and then, perhaps deciding the game was up, her observer turned and disappeared into the undergrowth.

For the rest of the day, Cathy thought about her lone watcher. Of course, they could simply have been walking and looking out to sea but for some reason, Cathy felt that this was not so. It was probably not that unexpected. It was a tight community. Surely any newcomer might be of interest, she supposed.

That day, following the odd incident of the figure on the moor, she felt unsettled. By evening time, she was acutely fearful of going to bed. Another night of lucid dreams seemed too awful to consider and with no alcohol in the cottage, she decided to walk the fifteen minutes to the village pub.

She hadn't spotted the pool table the last time she had been inside. It was at the far left of the bar, right at the back, and she found that if she followed the bar around, she made almost a complete circuit of the room. Towards the back was a dartboard that had seen better days and a cigarette-dispensing machine that Cathy thought must be some kind of antique.

The pub was reasonably quiet. Standing at the bar, she asked for a large glass of white wine. She heard Suzalinna's words of warning and frowned. She felt sure that something was wrong between them. Initially, Suzalinna had had her best interests at heart in booking this holiday and keeping tabs on her too. But at the back of her mind, Cathy had been harbouring a concern that her psychiatric consultant and Suzalinna might be discussing her progress informally without her there. It was unethical if they were because she hadn't given consent. It was a breach of her confidentiality. This thought had been running in her mind for the past few days. Maybe it was paranoia, but then again, perhaps it was intuition.

She took the first sip of wine and savoured it. She had seen that the pool table needed tokens, so got the attention of the girl at the bar once more and handed over a pound coin for two. She chalked her cue and took a few shots, finding herself moving onto her second glass of wine reasonably quickly. The pub was filling up. Some people had moved further around the bar to make room. She heard the door opening and closing, with shouts of recognition as more people arrived. Two men came to her side of the bar to move out of the way, and seeing her standing, cue in one hand, and a wine glass in the other, they laughed. The more interesting of the two offered to buy her a drink and challenged her to a game. His friend was reticent, and she saw him roll his eyes as he made his way back to the bar to collect their drinks.

'So, are you new around here?' the man asked.

'Just a flying visit really,' she said expansively, leaning on the pool table to steady herself. 'Staying at the farm cottages down the road.' She made a sweeping gesture as if to demonstrate the direction, but this might well have encompassed the whole of Kinnaven itself.

The man laughed. 'No way. My dad bloody owns those cottages. Look, that's my brother.' He pointed. 'He's your landlord. What a bit of luck.'

His brother returned with another token for the pool table, having overheard the end of the conversation. 'All right?' he asked. 'Alison said we had a new occupant. Hope everything's fine? Hi. Sorry, I'm Iain, nice to meet you. He's Ross, my annoying little brother. Don't fall for any of his crap. He's got a thousand lines and not one of them's true.'

Ross laughed and punched his brother on the arm. 'Ignore him. He's grouchy having been up half the night with the baby.'

'Oh, so she's had it then?' Cathy asked. 'I hadn't realised. Boy or girl?'

'Boy,' Iain answered and gulped his beer.

'I'm surprised you haven't been disturbed by the screaming

even down at the cottage. What a bloody racket when he gets going,' Ross said. 'Poor Alison's walking around like a zombie, and little wonder.' Cathy found herself transfixed by his beautiful eyes and slightly uneven, white teeth. Like a shark, she thought and grinned broadly at him.

'You've not told us your name,' Ross said.

Cathy told him and then tried very hard to look less drunk.

'So, you're staying in Kinnaven alone, Cathy?'

'All alone.' She nodded and grinned.

'Well, I'm only here to meet up with old friends and to get to know my new baby nephew now, of course. Hang on a minute.' Ross paused and then covered his mouth with his hand, apparently thinking. 'I do know you. I bumped into you the other day. Outside the chemist in the next town, I was picking up a prescription for Alison, my sister-in-law. You weren't looking where you were going and walked right into me. So, maybe it's fate us meeting twice, no?'

Cathy laughed again. She felt she could keep on laughing all evening.

'I might stay in Kinnaven for longer if there's a good reason,' Ross continued, raising an eyebrow. 'I grew up here, so maybe I can show you around a bit? Show you the sights?'

Cathy laughed again, not only at the predictability of his chat-up line but the irony. Kinnaven's sights? That wouldn't take them long. Still, though, it couldn't be denied that despite the fog of alcohol, her heart beat more rapidly at the thought of spending time with Ross. Perhaps things were looking up for her after all.

10

'S it down and tell me,' the old lady said to Jean when she'd finished vacuuming both upstairs and down. 'You know nothing shocks me these days. Something's amiss, I can tell. I've known you long enough to see these things.'

'Oh, Mrs Spratt,' she said, 'I don't know where to start.' Almost at once, Jean recognised Ross's own words and felt a little repulsed.

'Tea,' the old lady said definitely. 'I've biscuits in the tin. Some of the chocolate ones you like. I meant to get you to go into the cupboard to get a sweetie for Calum anyway. You know where they are.'

Jean went through to the kitchen and prepared a pot of tea, placing everything on a tray with a horrible illustration of faded home-grown vegetables. She opened the kitchen cupboard and retrieved the packet of fruit gums the old lady had bought for Calum and slipped them in her pocket. It was a habit Mrs Spratt had established, much to Jean's amusement, and she smiled at her thoughtfulness. As she was shutting the door, one of the old lady's hot water bottles fell, having been hung on a hook on the back of the door. In the past, Jean had chastised her for still using them, worrying Mrs Spratt might burn herself pouring the boiling water in.

Jean stooped and, replacing the bottle on the hook, felt something lumpy and unusual inside. Taking it down again and opening the cover, a knitted, striped affair in orange and mauve, Jean found herself looking at roll upon roll of carefully folded and banded banknotes. Her heart racing, she hurriedly closed the cover and hung the bottle once more on the door. This, she shut with a bang, wishing she had never looked in the first place, what with all of her troubles just now. Old people could be so foolish with their money, and what could the lady be thinking of keeping such an amount at home? It seemed preposterous to think her own little family was struggling daily to make ends meet and here the old lady had hoarded a small fortune with little likelihood of ever spending any of it either. She wondered if Mrs Spratt even remembered it was there. But it was none of her business.

When she returned to the living room, she immediately saw Mrs Spratt hadn't moved but was now resting her head awkwardly on her chair. As Jean approached, she saw the old lady's skin had become quite grey. Jean hurriedly put the tray down on the coffee table.

'Mrs Spratt, what on earth's the matter?'

The old lady's eyes opened. She tried to move her lips, but to Jean's horror, only the left side of the old woman's mouth lifted.

'Oh, Mrs Spratt! What's happened? I was only away a minute. I don't think you're very well.'

The old lady made a moaning sound and a small bubble emerged from her mouth. It rested lightly on her thin, now bluish, bottom lip.

'Mrs Spratt! I need to call the doctor. I think you're having a stroke.'

The old woman looked up at her wildly.

'No, don't panic. We'll get the doctor out. Dr Cosgrove will know what to do. You stay put and I'll call.'

She hurried into the hallway, closing the door behind her. With shaking hands, she attempted to find the surgery's number on her mobile, but repeatedly, she failed to press the correct buttons. *Stop panicking*, she told herself. *You're no use like this.* When she was finally in greater control, she was told by Frances, who answered the call, that the doctor would be along as soon as she was able.

Jean returned to the living room but was horrified to find the old lady was much worse. Now her torso seemed to have lost any tone and she leaned heavily to one side. Had the cushions, which Jean re-plumped, not been there, the old lady might have fallen from the chair completely.

'Oh God. Hurry up, Dr Cosgrove,' Jean moaned and then, more loudly: 'Not to worry, Mrs Spratt, she's on her way.'

The old woman had closed her eyes.

How long was the doctor going to be? She had phoned the surgery a good five minutes ago now. Perhaps she should call an ambulance but what if the doctor suddenly arrived and was annoyed? Would she be angry with her? Oh God, what should she do?

'I'll be back in a moment, Mrs Spratt,' Jean said to the now unhearing woman. She darted from the room again, out into the street, where she stood looking up and down, willing the doctor's car to appear. She stood helplessly for some minutes. 'Oh God,' she whimpered, and then returning to the house, she knew almost instantly that it was in vain. Her mother might have called it sixth sense. She had told Jean in the past they all had it, along with most of the women who came from that coastline. Jean stood silently in the hallway listening, afraid to go in and have her suspicions confirmed. Eventually, unable to put it off any longer, she called out to Mrs Spratt. Summoning her courage, she went in but the sense of finality hit her immediately.

Jean could feel the old lady all around her, a warm embrace encircling her as she sat down heavily on one of the armchairs to wait for the doctor, who was now too late.

'Oh, Mrs Spratt,' Jean whispered to herself. 'Poor, dear Mrs Spratt.'

She waited for some time, wringing her hands and weeping for the old lady who she had loved so dearly.

The doctor arrived half an hour later. Jean went to greet her at the door as the car pulled up.

'Morning, Jean,' the doctor said with a sympathetic smile. Jean had already called the practice once more to tell them it was now too late and the old lady had passed. Dr Cosgrove was clearly in a hurry. Jean felt slightly sickened by how easily she made the appropriate noises, being tactful as a doctor should, but Jean could tell her mind was elsewhere. It must be hard being a doctor and dealing with things like this, Jean told herself as she showed Dr Cosgrove inside. Hard to be everything to everyone and impossible to get it right all the time.

'You found her, did you? In doing your cleaning, were you? I didn't realise you worked for her too.'

'No. I didn't find her. I mean, it happened pretty much in front of me. All within a few minutes, perhaps no more than ten. I called you, but it was too late.'

Dr Cosgrove crossed the room and, as a matter of formality, took her stethoscope from her bag and listened to the old lady's chest for any signs of life remaining. Straightening up, she smiled at Mrs Spratt with, what Jean considered, a mildly patronising manner.

'Your time to go, wasn't it, Mrs Spratt?' the doctor said. 'She had a whole host of medical issues, so it's hardly a surprise.' She turned to Jean. 'Not unexpected at all. I'm sure she was glad to have a friendly face with her as she went.'

The old lady's skin was matt. A translucent grey paper. Even the wrinkles had begun to ease out. It gave her a more youthful look, strangely. Jean couldn't take her eyes off her old friend. 'I didn't think... I never knew, you see? Apart from her legs, I didn't think there was anything. I know she had those blood pressure pills and the ones for her kidneys, but she was so bright. She was cheery. We were about to have a cup of tea together. She was going to give me advice on my love life.'

The doctor smiled but was clearly unmoved. 'She was quite old. I don't think we need to worry about informing the procurator fiscal. She was an elderly lady, and it was her time to go. No close family then? I need to make a few quick calls.'

Jean nodded and listened as the doctor called through to the local undertakers.

'Can you wait with her a little longer?' the doctor asked, still holding the telephone, with her other hand cupped over the mouthpiece. Jean nodded. The doctor returned to the other person on the line and finally hung up. 'Someone from Robsons will be down in the next half hour to take her. I have to get on.'

Jean was running late herself but there was no alternative. Her other jobs would have to wait. She closed the door as the doctor left and went through to the kitchen, pouring the now cold pot of tea down the sink. *Oh God, what a thing to happen.*

Before the funeral directors arrived, she found herself hovering in the kitchen, unwilling to sit in the living room. She moved about the room restlessly and despite the terrible circumstances she found her eyes repeatedly drawn to the cupboard door. After what she had felt about Ross's indiscretion, she didn't know what she was thinking. Perhaps it was the shock. She thought of the money only feet away from her. Who would even know it was there? There were no close family and the old lady had loved her. Jean had done so much to help. Dear God, what was she contemplating though? She had always been trustworthy. Not once had she taken a thing from a client. She thought of Ross and the debt. He had been so distressed telling her about it. He had made a poor judgement. It seemed unfair that he should be caught and penalised just as he was trying to make a go of things. Jean's hands shook. They could return the money he had taken from the doctor. She considered Calum and the school trip he had been begging to go on but she couldn't afford.

She was in front of the cupboard and wouldn't have much time until the undertakers arrived. She would need to decide. Her heart quickened as she opened the door. It didn't mean she was taking anything. She was just looking and tidying the biscuits away. She hesitated, her hand on the hot water bottle cover. Without realising what was in it, someone clearing the house might easily throw it in the bin. But what was she thinking? Had Ross's influence on her turned her into this, stealing from a poor dead woman? Jean slipped her hand in the knitted cover that hung there and felt the roll of money between her fingers. *Just touching it*, she told herself. *Just touching.*

Hearing a car outside, Jean hastily withdrew her hand. Within it, she held a roll of the banknotes. In a panic, she slipped the money into her pocket and shut the cupboard door.

As she showed the undertakers through, a tall, stately-looking man, experienced in his job having seen death many a time before, nodded sympathetically. 'Must have been a bit of a shock finding her,' he said. 'We'll take care of the lady now, though. She's in safe hands.'

∼

It wasn't until that evening when at last Jean was able to see Ross and tell him about her appalling day. He made a fuss of her and when the full story emerged of not just the death of her favourite client but her dreadful error of judgement afterwards, he showed gratitude also, telling her he knew she had done it for the family as a whole and they need never mention the matter again. Ross wholeheartedly agreed the £200 that she had taken should, of course, be used to pay off his transgression at the surgery, something that could be done with sleight of hand by either of them. The rest, he said, should be kept aside for Calum. The school trip would be a wonderful surprise for him as Jean had already expressed her difficulty in affording such a luxury. Ross also suggested setting up a child trust fund, so that, if in the future there was any spare, they might give Calum a better start in life than themselves. And so, with Ross's support, Jean gradually came to accept what she had done.

Their relationship was, in her opinion, the best it had ever been during those days following Mrs Spratt's death. Ross suggested the three of them should take a trip to Aberdeen at the weekend. Calum had been talking about a film he had wanted to see. Usually, it would be too excessive to manage but Ross said they should allow the poor kid a few treats now and then, and Jean herself deserved to get out of the village also after the week she had had.

'I was up at the farm today cleaning,' Jean said to Ross. They sat side-by-side watching Calum across the aisle as he gazed excitedly out of the train window. Occasionally the young boy would smile back at them and giggle if the train moved in a jauntier manner.

'Oh?' said Ross. 'And what was new? Did you see the baby? He was screaming the house down when I was in and Alison was making a hash of trying to feed him. I honestly think there's something not quite right with her. Really off with me, she was.

I'm glad to have your place to crash at now. They need the space anyway, and we most certainly do. I feel like a different man since I've been holed up with you half the week.' He nudged her in the ribs and Jean giggled.

'Yes, I have to say, I agree. Alison looked exhausted and on edge. But who wouldn't be with a new baby? I was glad not to walk in and find someone dead or dying.' She looked at Ross and he grinned. 'Alison's got a new holiday let staying. A young woman from near Ayr or the Borders, I think. A doctor, I believe. Beautiful, but jumpy, you know? She said she was there to convalesce, whatever that means. Very tidy, though. I hardly had to clean a thing when I was in.'

'Mental case, most likely,' Ross said and turned to look across at the little boy again.

Had Jean been more observant, she might have seen the flicker of apprehension in Ross's beautiful eyes at the mention of the woman, but she was far too distracted by the excitement of the journey to notice a thing.

11

D r Cosgrove arrived early, as she always did. She was keen to get seated in her pew at the front to avoid the gaggle of dreadful women at the church door. She had no interest in joining in with the local gossip and chit-chat. Sundays were her days to do with as she pleased. A day of rest and reflection, not conversation and queries about Mrs Higgins' chilblains. What a week it had been.

Now, she sat with her hands folded neatly in her lap. Her back was upright and uncomfortable against the cold wood. She turned slightly, adjusting herself, and noticed the burgundy cushions along some of the benches needed replacing. Worn and threadbare. In some places, the foam padding had become exposed. The minister didn't have an eye for detail these days. He had let things slide.

He had greeted her briefly as she came in. Their relationship was so well established that little had to be said. She knew he had a job to do, just as she had hers. He could mould himself into the person his parishioner needed. Educated, silent wisdom for her, perhaps jovial humour for the likes of the ageing women in their Sunday frocks. Voices wafted down the aisle now, echoing around the small church, looking for a place to land. A peel of laughter rang out. Dr Cosgrove recognised the voice and sat deeper in her seat, hoping to be spared.

It was so often this way. A time to reflect on her week and to consider how she might have done things differently. Ruth had been on her mind a good deal since Friday. If truth be told, along with the letters, she had thought of little else. While she sat waiting for the service to begin, Dr Cosgrove thought of her partner and prayed they might find some common ground once more after their minor fall out two days before. It had been so trivial after all, and in many ways the weekend had come at the wrong time. Had it been mid-week, they might have sorted the whole thing the following day. Instead, Dr Cosgrove imagined her poor dear friend worrying over the matter all weekend just as she had done. So silly.

Dr Cosgrove had had a busy morning that Friday. She had failed to catch Ruth the previous day as her partner had been out at a trainers' meeting. Dr Cosgrove had ably manned the fort along with the salaried GP. She had gone into the young woman's room and had pulled her up on the missed appendicitis. 'Not a big deal,' the old doctor had said to her. 'Just to flag it up as a learning opportunity for yourself.' The salaried GP had blushed and nodded. Dr Cosgrove had smiled as she had left her room. 'You're doing a grand job otherwise,' she had reassured her. 'I know Ruth is very happy with you,' and she had shut the door.

When she did finally manage to grab Ruth, they were both rushed.

'Ruth?' Dr Cosgrove had called from behind reception where she stood. She had been discussing something with one of the reception girls and came around to join her colleague.

'Oh sorry, Heather, I need to dash. I've got two to write up and someone's been trying to call me on my mobile all the way while I was driving back. Was it urgent?'

Dr Cosgrove waved her colleague an understanding acknowledgement. 'I'll pop in in five minutes,' she said to Ruth's rapidly retreating figure.

When she entered Ruth's room, her colleague looked more composed.

'Heather,' Ruth had said, getting up and closing the door behind her. 'Sorry about that. Like fighting fire with fire this morning. What was it you wanted to say? Is everything all right?'

Dr Cosgrove had told her there were a couple of things she had wanted to discuss. Nothing urgent or worrying, of course. She mentioned the death of old Mrs Spratt in the village and explained about the case from a few days back: the abdominal pain their salaried GP had imprudently sent home. 'It was as well the patient came in the following day to see me,' Dr Cosgrove explained. 'I phoned Surgical this morning to see how she was doing. They operated. Appendicitis, of course. Both you or I would have known that, had we seen her the first day.'

Ruth had looked puzzled. 'I don't quite see your point though, Heather. I take it she followed it up with a caveat that if the girl's symptoms worsened, she should return to the practice? It's all very well knowing in hindsight, but I don't think it's such a grave error of judgement myself. Abdos can be ambiguous, to say the least.'

Dr Cosgrove bristled slightly. 'I had a word with her yesterday morning,' she said. 'I thought it best. Now, another thing. I wanted to ask if you had taken anything from the petty cash the other day?'

Ruth's eyebrows had shot up. 'No. No, I haven't. What's this about?'

'Nothing to concern yourself over. Just a little staffing matter. I thought I would check before taking it any further. Leave it with me,' Dr Cosgrove had said, seeing her partner glancing at her computer screen. 'And one last thing,' she said, knowing they would be unlikely to talk again all day. 'I wanted to discuss the retirement briefly. I've had an idea.'

The conversation had not ended well. Dr Cosgrove, feeling she had not been fully understood, had left the room in high dudgeon. She and Ruth rarely argued. There had been the odd incident, but nothing to speak of. It felt frightful. But as the day continued, she felt this would surely pass and Ruth would come to her senses. They would talk later when Ruth had calmed down. Perhaps it had been a bad time. Ruth had been harassed and bothered already that morning. Let it lie. Let it be.

The old minister walked through the body of the church now, his footsteps echoing along the pews. Composed and in position, he smiled short-sightedly around the church. 'Welcome, welcome.' It was fascinating to watch him speak. For the first time in many weeks, possibly months, Dr Cosgrove considered the man, doing clearly what he was destined to do, and still, after all these years, loving his job. Perhaps they were not so different, really. She had found her vocation young, as he had. It had taken them both in a direction which led to fulfilment, yet solitude.

It had almost happened for her. There had been an understanding, not quite a romance even. Dr Cosgrove guarded her near-attachment with fond but slightly removed nostalgia. She wondered where he was now. A unity, nearly, but not quite. The pain of the lost connection was far less intense than forty years ago, but she still didn't choose to dwell on it. Her father had disapproved. The individual hadn't been a doctor. It was rather complicated. But she knew her father had been right. Better to step away at that time, than to be drawn further into what could potentially be a mistake. She wondered about the minister and his situation. Having never considered it before, her mind wandered and she found she had barely heard any of what he had said these last few minutes. She must concentrate.

They sang the customary chosen hymn. Dr Cosgrove always sang loud and clear, as if her voice might lift the rest. She had been told to do so by her father as a girl. Behind her came the frail unsteady bleats of the elderly women, accompanied by the lower faltering tones of their husbands. She smiled a little as she heard the minister losing himself a couple of times in the third verse and humming along to the creaking organ instead.

He spoke with force and vigour and as she sat there, Dr Cosgrove only then became aware of her father sitting to the left and behind. He had been present more often of late. She glanced twice over her shoulder but he raised a hand as if to remonstrate. Dr Cosgrove returned her attention to the minister once more. She tried to listen but stole another look around to him. He did not acknowledge her and was now sitting with his head bowed.

A child at the back of the church began to cry, interrupting the sermon and providing some relief to the bewildered audience. Only Dr Cosgrove had truly understood the minister's words and their deeper meaning. After all, the entire sermon had been spoken wholly to her. Her father had marched from the church as the final hymn was being sung. Dr Cosgrove wanted to follow but knew he would not allow it.

Unfortunately, she was unable to navigate the Kinnaven gossips quickly enough that morning after the service. Eventually, she extricated herself and marched homewards. She was almost at the foot of the hill when she was forced to slow down again. Ahead of her walked a couple pushing a pram. Presumably, they were responsible for the baby who had been crying in the church earlier. She was quite a distance behind them but didn't think she had seen them before. The wife, for she assumed, rather outdatedly, that anyone with a child should be married, was talking animatedly as her husband pushed the pram. She thought they were arguing. The woman was gesturing in anger. Dr Cosgrove smiled sadly. A difficult time.

When she finally arrived home, opening the door wide and calling out to him, she was met by a stony silence. Before even removing her shoes, she walked quickly into the living room. It was empty. The house felt cold and unwelcoming.

It took her most of the afternoon to settle. She worried about the sermon and the couple she had followed down the road. The woman had looked at her oddly as she passed. When she thought about it, the gossips had been too vocal today as well. Mrs Spratt's name had been mentioned. Did they blame her for not saving the old woman? Something wasn't right. And then there was her father, not waiting. All that afternoon, she worried. Come evening time, she was finally rested in her armchair reading, when she looked up and he was with her.

'Where's Mother?' she asked, but he didn't answer. He rarely did.

His lack of words enraged her at times, but it had always been so. He continued to pace the room. His figure, still upright and principled. His features, although pale now, were as distinct as ever. She watched him for some time, her book lying in her lap, her tea untouched. She had no idea how long she sat. Eventually, she spoke once more.

'Please,' she begged him, but he was resolute and would not be drawn. 'Please, Father.'

12

It was about a week after Mrs Spratt's death and following the funeral, when Jean finally snapped. The plan had been to return the money taken from the doctor's deposit box. She had entrusted this task to Ross, given that it was his mistake to correct, and anyway, he was working behind the front reception desk and his presence there would be less obvious than hers. He had all but told her that on the first day of returning to work following their weekend trip to Aberdeen, he had rectified his mistake. Only on Friday did she discover this to be untrue.

It was early morning, and before doctors' surgeries started, Jean cleaned the sinks and lavatories and vacuumed the waiting area, having already seen to the consulting rooms the night before. Frances and the other receptionist, Anita, were already there. Frances was having a bad start to the day. As Jean tidied the magazines in the waiting room and moved two chairs to their rightful position in line with the rest, she heard Frances' voice high-pitched and imploring from behind the desk.

'But I was sure,' she said.

Jean heard another voice, soothing and reasoning, telling her to look again. She must be mistaken.

Sudden nausea swept over Jean, but she continued with her work, her head down, knowing that soon the patients and doctors would arrive and she would need to be out. It was only as she was leaving that the truth came out. She had gone to the back door to collect her jacket and to change out of her tabard, which she wore when using bleach. Too many times she had returned home to find her jeans or T-shirts had been spattered and faded with splash-back. As she was opening the fire exit to leave, a practice common amongst the staff as the door led directly to the car park, Frances appeared, breathless and clearly upset.

'Oh, Jean,' she said, 'I was going to the bathroom. I'm in a state and the day's not even started.'

Jean paused, her hand on the metal bar of the emergency door. 'What's wrong?' she asked, desperately wanting to leave without knowing.

'The kitty,' Frances said. 'It doesn't add up. I know I put the money in, but it's gone and Dr Cosgrove's going to be furious when she finds out.'

'What money?' Jean lied and was horrified at how sympathetic she sounded. 'Why is there money in a doctors' surgery anyway?'

'Oh, it wasn't that much, but when we charge patients for letters and forms, we put it in the deposit box and I'm meant to take the thing to the bank. Of course, it was Michael's birthday this weekend and I was tied up with that.'

Jean nodded. Michael was a couple of years below Calum in school and she knew the family. 'Are you sure it was there in the first place? I'm only saying because I was convinced I had forty pounds the other day when in fact I only had ten in my purse. It was my mistake, of course.' Jean felt sick at having concocted this half-truth. She had indeed lost thirty pounds and the disappearance was still to be explained, but she had a fair idea where it had gone and it was much the same way as the doctors' money.

'Anita said that too. She said I'd added it up wrong, but I was sure and I even remember the patient. He was a pig to me and Zoe when she was on the desk that afternoon. Your friend, Ross, was with us. He overheard and stuck up for us a bit.'

Jean nodded. 'I hope you sort it out. Dr Cosgrove's not as bad as all that, is she?'

Frances smiled thinly. 'Sometimes she is, and sometimes not. She's got a lot on her mind lately with her impending retirement and she's not been herself at all. Let's hope the money turns up or she forgets about it soon.'

When Jean arrived at her next job down at the farm holiday lets, she was close to hysteria. How could Ross have been so foolish? Why hadn't he returned the money immediately? Why had he lied to her again? The woman, who Jean now knew was called Cathy, saw her distress at once and, against her better judgement, Jean found herself sitting at the kitchen table, venting. For Jean, this didn't feel entirely comfortable. Drinking tea with a stranger and telling her woes, albeit a highly edited version, felt odd. But then, who else could she tell?

'Just have it out with him,' Cathy had said. 'Whatever's bothering you needs to be out in the open. I know you're worried about this boy of yours and afraid to rock the boat in case it ends, but isn't it better to find out now, before things get more serious?'

Of course, Cathy was right. Jean had been careful not to mention names in case they came across one another at the farm, but she hoped she could employ some of Cathy's advice and stay firm. The young doctor was, after all, very astute, that was clear for Jean to see.

While she waited for Ross to return from seeing his father, she considered Cathy: the fragile, pale doctor staying alone in the holiday lets. Jean wondered why she was convalescing. While she had spoken with her, Jean had quite forgotten what Alison had said about her being in the medical profession, and, at times during the conversation, Jean felt that she, despite her worries over Ross, was the more robust of the two.

Looking up, she saw a shadow at the window. She was determined to maintain her self-control even when she saw Ross's casual swagger as he came up the driveway and his slow smile as he saw her at the window watching for him. When he came in, scooping up Calum in his arms and calling her 'honey' and 'darling', she could contain herself no more.

'Look, Jeanie,' he implored, 'I've just come in and it's been some day too.' He bent down to Calum and ruffled his hair. 'Grab the football, bud, I've got a new trick to teach you after your grumpy mum's had it out with me. Keepy-ups until I escape, okay?'

The young boy disappeared out into the backyard.

'I wish you wouldn't speak like that in front of him,' Jean said. 'Anyway, about the money. What have you got to say? I thought you'd replaced it and today I find out it was a lie.'

'Oh, Jean. Listen, I never said I'd put it back, and I did try, but that silly receptionist was buzzing around half the time and I didn't get a chance.'

'Well, she's probably been fired by now because of it. Almost in tears, she was. If you thought you were going to struggle to replace it, you might have given it to me. I was in there and could have made some excuse to go cleaning behind the desk. I was even alone the night before when I was doing the doctors' rooms. I could have done it then.'

'I'd never have allowed you to get involved. The old doctor won't think twice about the money after a day or so, and the office girl won't lose her job over a simple mistake. Why would she? Darling, Jean, it'll all be fine. You wait and see.'

'But when are you going to return the money, Ross? I thought that was the plan. That's why I took Mrs Spratt's money, to replace what you had taken.'

Ross walked towards her and taking her by the shoulders, he kissed the top of her head. 'Darling, that's not quite true though, is it?' He tucked a strand of hair behind her ear. 'We enjoyed a lovely trip to Aberdeen together, and then there's Calum's school outing too. Honestly, honey, if you say you took it to cover for me, then you're fooling no one but yourself. Oh, Jean, don't look so cross. I love you for doing it. You made me proud and after I've put that beautiful son of yours into bed, I'll show you how proud I am.'

Ross pressed his lips to hers and kissed her so deeply and passionately that she was quite shaken.

'It's all for you, darling,' he whispered, inches from her face. His breath was warm on her wet mouth. 'I'll explain everything. I have a plan, but remember, it's always only been for you.'

Then pulling back, he was himself once more. He looked down at her roguishly, perhaps seeing that he had put her off guard. His lopsided smile made him look younger than his years, and Jean knew she was blushing.

'Later,' he said firmly, and then turned and followed her son into the garden.

Jean was left with her thoughts. She had checked the bank balance that afternoon and had been horrified to see her savings were all but gone. It had been foolish of her, of course, but the offer of marriage had made her lose sight of things. She had thought that what she had was his. And now, she had placed herself, and more importantly her son, in jeopardy. What did Ross mean by a plan? Part of her felt that she should have kicked him out of the house there and then, but she was undeniably in love with him and, if truth be told, she always had been, even during her marriage to Daniel. She bit her tongue until the evening when they were free to speak in private.

'I've got an idea,' Ross said, when they were finally alone, Calum having been sent to bed with promises of more football practice the following day.

'What is it?' she asked unhappily.

'Oh, sweetheart, don't,' he said in protest. 'Is this what it's come to? Have I reduced you to this? I need your support. You're the only one, you see? No one else understands. No one else knows what I've seen. The horror of it all. I can't tell you how hard it's been since I came back. So many memories and then there are the nightmares.'

To Jean's dismay, tears appeared in his eyes.

'Oh, Ross!' She was now close to tears herself. 'It's been hard for me too. I'm not a bad person and these last few days, I've felt so guilty for what I've done. All I ever wanted was to be with you. I'm no good at all of this, you know I'm not.'

'You're a good person. Too good for me, that's why and I shouldn't ask you. You should send me away now and we'll say no more, Jean. No hard feelings. I'll always be a friend to you, but if you've had enough, and I wouldn't blame you, then we should call it time. It's not fair on Calum, me and him getting close. I'll never regret coming back to you, but I love you so much, I'd walk away now to save you from harm.'

Jean couldn't help herself and they kissed, with Ross holding her head in his hands and her leaning into him completely.

'Darling,' he said eventually, breathing heavily. 'I told you I had a plan, but I'm not sure how to begin. You'll not like it but if you meant what you said, that you and I were forever, then it's the only way. I want to set up home together properly, but on our wages, there's just no way. I know I've more to explain too. I couldn't bring myself to do it before, but this army nonsense has caught up with me a bit. That's why I've been so off at times. I told you about the blackmail, but one of the lads has found out where I am and he's threatening to tell my dad. You know what that might mean. No inheritance. If Dad found out I was messing around with drugs, he'd write me out of the will immediately. Things are so good between us now; I can't allow that to happen. The lad says he'll leave it alone if I give him a grand. Oh God, Jean, I know! You don't need to look like that, but once it's paid, we'd be free and then we can enjoy our life together. You can see that, can't you?'

'But once this money's paid, he'll ask you for more, don't you see? That's what blackmailers do. Why can't we live as we have been? I know it's tight every month but we love each other enough for it not to matter. We don't need your inheritance at all.'

Ross took her left hand in his and taking the fourth finger, kissed it. 'Jeanie, no. Not you. You deserve better and so does that beautiful son of yours, of ours, Jean. You know I take the full package when I say I want you. It's Calum as well. I love that kid like he's my own. He deserves better than living hand to mouth, we all do.'

Jean nodded slowly. 'Well?' she asked. 'What's this plan?'

'It's hard to know where to start, really it is, but hear me out and then you can say no and put an end to this madness.'

Jean smiled.

'My idea is to be married next year,' he began. 'That's if you'll have me, but first, we need capital. You know all of this is coming to me in the future. You must remember that always, Jean. My father will undoubtedly leave me half of the farm and then I'll repay you a thousand times over and more for your trust and kindness.'

'You know I'm not interested in your money, Ross.' She laughed.

'No, of course, darling. But to tide us over until then, we need to do something drastic. You saw how easy it was to acquire a small amount from Mrs Spratt...'

Jean grimaced.

'I know it was unpleasant, but in doing what you did, you proved to me you had guts. And so, I feel able to ask you again. You are in an unusually advantageous position doing what you do, you know?'

Jean was confused. 'What, cleaning?'

Ross laughed. 'Exactly. I know I poured scorn on your job when I first came back, but what you've done in setting up a business and grafting away day in, day out, building up a list of clients, well, that takes guts and stamina, darling.'

'So, what's this got to do with us earning money?' she asked. 'I can't take on any more jobs and if you're proposing working alongside me, then forget it. I've seen how lazy you can be. You can't even put the toilet seat down after going, let alone clean the pan.'

'I don't like this any more than you, but it's the only way. We're both of us in this thing already, what with the doctor's money and then your little indiscretion with Mrs Spratt. What harm would it do to very carefully select a few others? Clients of yours that you know wouldn't miss it. I'm not talking about the old dears, but the well-off ones.' Ross paused as if gauging how his idea fell on her.

'It's horrible, Ross! Utterly awful. You want me to steal from my trusted customers? Is that what you suggest?'

'I know, darling. It's an unpleasant thing to say. Truly, I've gone over and over it in my head, trying to think of a different way. But listen, it might not necessarily be money. Perhaps information. I'm not clear until we begin. Once we've made a list of possible candidates, we'll go through the details. Other than that, we need never speak of it. I know it sickens you. But all the while, a little money here or there would soon add up. Just imagine. We'd have enough to pay off this man and to marry. Just think of it, Jeanie. Soon all of our troubles will be gone.'

Jean allowed him to kiss her once more, but this time, she attempted to withhold a little. She knew there could be no going back if she accepted him. Already, despite herself, she was floundering. Before long, she would be completely lost.

13

When he arrived at the cottage, Cathy found herself more than a little flustered. Her drunken encounter with Ross had been on her mind a good deal since that evening. Strangely, she felt embarrassed but rather liberated by the experience. Nothing had happened that night, of course.

Ross, as he kissed her lightly on the cheek after walking her to her door, might well have been persuaded though, she thought. She had concluded that it had been a nice distraction from her troubles. And why not? She was single. She was a grown woman. She was entitled to flirt with anyone she chose. Several times that following week, she recollected images of herself walking, or rather stumbling, down the farm track, with Ross's arm steadying her, their fingers interlinked. Opening the door that morning though, she had certainly not expected the subject of her romantic musings to be grinning in front of her.

He stood in the doorway, his tall figure blocking the seascape behind. Her eyes moved down from his crooked smile to his faded jeans and T-shirt which caught and billowed behind him in the wind. Finally then, to his hands, in which he held what looked like a plastic doctor's bag.

'The kitchen,' he said, as if this might explain. But when she still looked confused, his smile broadened. 'Alison said you'd got a loose hinge? She told me to look at it and the slats in the airing cupboard. Your cleaner said the whole shelf is unstable and Alison is afraid of you being crushed under an avalanche of freshly laundered towels.'

Cathy smiled. 'Of course.' She stepped aside. It was foolish of her to think he had come back to see her for any other reason.

Ross moved through the cottage, and she found herself making small talk to fill the awkwardness of the situation, although he seemed completely at home. He began in the kitchen, placing, what was obvious to her now, a toolbox, on the kitchen worktop.

'So,' he said as he began to work, opening the cupboard she indicated as being the problem and crouching down to see better. 'How have you been, Cathy? You've been on my mind, as it happens.' He looked up from his current squatting position and met her gaze, holding it for slightly too long. His eyes were serious, but then raising his right eyebrow, she saw he was teasing and she smiled.

'I bet you say that to all of the girls. Do you want tea? I'm making some for myself.'

Over the next hour, they chatted about Kinnaven and about how it had been as a child growing up in the tiny village. He told her about his father's disappointment in him not wanting to take on the farm, but that his older brother had done so instead. It had left a strain between them. The bad feeling had even extended to his sister-in-law also, and he often felt out on a limb up in the old farmhouse that was once his childhood home. He said he always felt like the black sheep of the family and his father had never really forgiven him for leaving the place. More than anything, he said he wanted to gain his father's respect but doubted that he ever could. They spoke about his travels and of the countries he had visited while in the army. He had seen many things and had experienced so much, but some of what he had witnessed had left its mark. He told her he had established some great friendships in the army all the same. The sense of camaraderie had kept him going even during the bleakest of times. Wherever he travelled to though, he always felt a little bit of him was lost. That was why he had returned. To find his missing piece. He felt sure it was here in Kinnaven.

'And what should I find returning home, but you?' He laughed. 'Fate, you see? I told you that before. Why else would we have met?'

Cathy laughed. 'You have all the lines.'

That morning, she felt like a passive sounding board to his conversation. She listened to him with genuine interest, occasionally making a remark, asking a question to clarify, or simply nodding in assent and allowing him to speak.

'I've never met anyone like you,' he said at one point, and for all of his corny lines, she believed it.

When he had finished his work, they found themselves sitting out at the front of the cottage on the doorstep, nursing their mugs of tea and balancing biscuits on their knees, just as Cathy had done alone so many times before. In truth, Ross had surprised her. He had originally seemed quite one-dimensional, but there was so much more. She had imagined him as a bit of a player, but perhaps she'd been wrong.

'You must love coming back to all of this,' she said, gazing out at the water. When he didn't answer, she turned. He seemed absent. His eyes were far away, their deep blue as cold as the sea itself. She didn't ask again, knowing that to do so would only break the spell, but wondered what memory he relived as a shadow of almost childlike sorrow crossed his countenance. When finally, he roused himself, he seemed to have completely lost his light-heartedness.

'Well? What's happened?' she finally asked him, unsure if in doing so, she might provoke anger or upset.

Ross smiled. He touched his bottom lip to let her know she had a crumb clinging to her own. She wafted a hand, and missing the offending fragment, he removed it for her. Although he smiled, his eyes were serious.

'A whole lot of stuff happened this morning.' He sighed and looked at her as if trying to decide if he should speak. 'My brother's wife.' He took a sip of his tea and grimaced. 'I wasn't going to say. I've already said too much today. I don't know why. Maybe you're easy to speak to. A good listener.'

Cathy didn't answer. Perhaps he was right. Perhaps they had both let their guard down too much.

He turned and seemed to be battling some inner turmoil. 'Cathy, you're a doctor, aren't you?' He looked keenly at her now, his eyes dark. She nodded her head slightly.

His story was hesitant, but he continued, intermittently crumbling the edge of his biscuit between his forefinger and thumb.

'From what he says, Iain, I mean, she's always been a bit uptight. Maybe I shouldn't be saying this. I mean, it's actually no more my business than yours, but Iain and I are brothers, for all of our differences, you see? I'm concerned.' Ross again looked out to sea. 'I went up there this morning, to the farmhouse. I've been trying to give them space. I'm staying at a friend's in the village and keeping out of their hair as much as possible since the baby arrived. I know it was always going to be a stressful time for them. Of course, it goes without saying. Things have been awkward for some time, though. From what Iain says, it was turbulent before Alison was even pregnant. Since I arrived, it's worsened. I've probably put a greater strain on things. Anyway, I shouldn't have expected anything less, to be fair. I've been out of my brother's, well, my whole family's life, for a long

94

time now. I thought she'd be more relaxed, though. We've hardly met in the past, but when we have, she's been nice enough. She and I got on like a house on fire at Mum's funeral nearly a year back. But she's just had the baby, and anyway, things have been seriously odd.' Ross looked at Cathy again, perhaps checking that she was still following.

'This morning,' he said. He took a moment and looked at her more closely for the first time since beginning his monologue. 'Sorry, I'm going on a bit, aren't I?'

Cathy laughed. 'No different to my Tuesday morning surgery at the practice.' But she immediately regretted her joke. 'Not funny. I'm sorry, go on.'

'So, Iain says that Alison's been getting edgy about things. We had wanted to go for a walk around the village the other day. We were going to take the baby to give her a break for a bit. It was meant to be a favour. Anyway, she went nuts. Ran upstairs with the baby, didn't want us to leave. Iain's told me she's been crying while she feeds him. I don't know anything about that kind of thing but she's sitting feeding and she'll start crying for no reason. That can't be normal, can it? She's seen someone at the health centre about it already.'

Cathy made a non-committal noise and signalled for him to continue.

'So, today, I went in to say good morning before coming here and Iain was in a right state about things. He said she had gone missing earlier and taken the baby too. Seriously, he was apparently in a total panic at the time. Went tearing around the house calling for her and then finally, he found her.' Ross paused and again looked directly at her. 'Cathy, she was standing on the clifftop, just along from here.'

'What? With the baby? When was this?'

'Early in the morning, so Iain says. He found her. Just standing there, on the cliffs looking out to sea, holding the baby.

I mean Cathy, that's scary. What was she going to do? Iain thinks she was going to throw herself off.'

'Well, that's a bit dramatic. It does sound as if she needs to speak to someone, but did he have any reason to think she was suicidal?'

'It was five in the morning, Cathy. She was hardly out for a stroll.'

'No, but it sounds like your brother's got a bit stressed about things. Maybe he needs to be talking to someone too.'

Ross looked away and she knew it wasn't enough. He wasn't happy at all.

'Well, I can only go on what you've told me,' she said. 'It's hard when you're hearing it second- or third-hand. I'm no psychiatrist anyway,' she finished and could have added that she could hardly class herself as a bloody doctor anymore for that matter, but she left it. It wasn't a good resolution to the situation, and although Ross nodded, she knew he still wasn't satisfied, but they spoke of it no more.

When he had to go, he told her he wanted to see her again, to take her up to the next town, even that afternoon if she was free. He said he'd cancel his work, do anything to make it happen. Cathy hesitated. She hadn't come to Kinnaven for this, and really, she was in no position to be considering it. She was no fool though, and supposed that the fact that she was only visiting made her a more attractive proposition to Ross. She thanked him but told him she had plans. He looked crestfallen but said he hoped to bump into her in the pub again for a game of pool. That was fine, she thought. Better to keep people at a distance. It was safer that way.

All afternoon, Ross's story of Alison on the clifftops played on her mind. Not for the first time, she felt that something was very wrong with that family. She repeatedly tortured herself with her lack of tact in dealing with Ross and her failure generally. What was wrong with her? After years of training, she should be able to advise without offending. Perhaps she was losing it completely. The illness had taken her ability to empathise. It should have been the other way around. Having seen things from the patient's point of view, she should be more understanding. What did that make her then?

Cathy paced the small living room to the cottage, her feet treading the same path across the patterned carpet. Back and forth. And what had Ross thought of her? She had come across as cold and uncaring. Heartless, that was what she was. Cathy shook her head in disgust. What was she doing fooling around like this anyway? She barely knew the guy so why did it matter so much? If she ever intended on returning to work, this was hardly the right way to go about it. She paused mid-step and thought of the practice, its harled white walls and red roof. At the door, the brass sign. She smiled involuntarily seeing her name engraved below her partners: 'Dr Cathy Moreland MBChB MRCGP'. The pride that first day, of walking through the doctors' corridor, past the waiting room, coming finally to her room. Her own consulting room, that she had thoughtlessly gone in and out of daily, even moaning sometimes about the monotony of the routine and the burden of the workload.

Cathy grimaced and covered her ears with her hands. *Oh, God! Make it stop.* A week into her stay in Kinnaven and what progress had she made? An image of her psychiatrist's face flashed before her, his sad, insipid smile, his pen hovering over her notes. Of course, he knew that she'd never return to work. This had all been an exercise to dampen the blow. And Suzalinna too. Cathy had seen her and the psychiatrist talking quietly before she left the hospital. She could imagine the hushed words now. 'Perhaps, let it sink in slowly... Seems unlikely but let's not destroy her hopes... Safety of her patients is paramount...' Suzalinna had glanced towards her across the ward, a look of pity, of course. She had seen it at the time but hadn't realised why.

By mid-afternoon, she found herself contemplating the unthinkable. *Just one*, she remonstrated. It would take the edge off things and lift her, even for a short while. Alcohol was of no use to her and she knew that it would be so quick and easy. The relief of even touching the packet would be immense. She held the morphine sulphate in her hand and turned it over again and again in her palm. Only one. One would not make a difference to the overall picture. Just one.

She sat in the living room, propped up in an armchair. It would come soon enough. Slowly, she felt her brow relax. Her mind was empty. Her jaw became heavy and her arms were like lead. She allowed herself to be swallowed by it. Cool waves lapped over her. The release was vast and expansive. She drifted and fell gracefully this time. There was no hard concrete or shingle on which to land, only merciful smoothness. Her lips were dry, and she licked them, tasting sweetness. She went with it and lost herself entirely.

14

D r Cosgrove removed her spectacles. 'Of course, I'm only too happy to help,' she said.

Cathy shifted awkwardly in her seat. 'I should have made sure,' she repeated. 'You'd have thought I, of all people, would know better.'

'It's not a bother to me,' the other doctor reassured. 'If you have the packet, I'll do a prescription now. What practice did you say you worked for again?'

'Glainkirk. It's in the Borders. Nice. Semi-rural. I've been a partner for five or six years. The bipolar came as a blow.' Cathy's voice wavered as she said the last sentence.

Dr Cosgrove looked up. Her eyes were slightly clouded and full of sympathy.

Cathy blushed and studied her hands. *Don't cry in front of a stranger*, she begged herself. *Just get through the consultation and out the other end.* She pulled at a ragged bit of skin next to one of her fingernails. It stung and she saw the flush of crimson as the capillary opened. She pressed her thumb on it and looked up once more.

The other doctor was nodding. 'It's hard,' she said. 'I can

imagine. Being on the other side of things as a patient is humbling. We all need help from time to time, though. It's not a crime. I'm very fortunate. I've been spared anything of the sort, but it doesn't mean I don't understand. Do they think you'll get back to work, the psychiatrists, I mean?'

Cathy swallowed. 'Too soon to say. I hope...'

Dr Cosgrove smiled. 'Yes, well, you've chosen a nice place to recuperate. A bit of sea air, some bracing walks. Just what the doctor ordered. That's an old-fashioned prescription, but one I recommend fully.'

Cathy brought out the nearly-empty packet of medication and placed it on the desk. 'It's just one tablet in the morning now I'm on the maintenance dose.'

Dr Cosgrove pulled the packet closer to her. 'Ari-pip-razole,' she read slowly. 'Not one I know too well. Is it a new antipsychotic? Most of my bipolars are on lithium.'

'Not that new,' Cathy said. Her hands were trembling. Dr Cosgrove had already begun to write. Should she chance it? She reached into her pocket once again. 'I wonder if you'd be able to do my pain medication at the same time too?'

Dr Cosgrove looked up from her prescription pad.

Cathy blushed. 'A long-standing issue, on and off. I have hypermobile joints and I find the dihydrocodeine helps when I get a partial subluxation.' Her heart was drumming in her ears. She swallowed. 'It's usually my shoulder. If you'd rather not, it's fine. I just thought...'

Dr Cosgrove lifted the packet of dihydrocodeine and studied it. Cathy had deliberately removed it from the outer box, which stated that it was Glainkirk Practice stock. A parting gift to herself before she took her things and left. She was filled with self-disgust even thinking about what she had done.

The ticking of the clock on the wall seemed deafening. She was about to speak once more, but Dr Cosgrove had decided.

'Obviously, considering the history of mental health and the fact that you're here alone...'

'It's fine,' Cathy said. 'I didn't expect...' Saliva pooled in her mouth. If only she could get outside.

But Dr Cosgrove wasn't finished. 'Now, as you're a medical professional, you know the risks.'

Oh God, not a lecture.

'These strong opiates are so addictive. Not a first-line choice. Of course, I'm not suggesting anything of the sort in your case. Some of my lesser clientele might well be tempted though...'

'Please, forget it. I still have two tablets,' Cathy begged. 'Forget I even asked. I can see your difficulty. You don't know me from Adam. I could be any old drug addict, for all you know.'

Dr Cosgrove placed the packet down on the desk with a snap. 'Yes, well...' She adjusted her glasses once more. 'Always tricky,' she said to herself and nodded. Her pen hovered above the prescription pad. 'The two tablets will presumably see you through until you can...'

'Absolutely.'

She had signed the thing. Two weeks supply of her antipsychotic only. Cathy's fingers twitched in her lap. If only she'd hand the prescription over and let her leave.

Dr Cosgrove pushed back her chair. 'It's been a pleasure,' she said, still holding the paper.

Cathy stood also. 'Thank you.' She held out her hand for the prescription.

But Dr Cosgrove misunderstood and stepped forward to shake it.

'Oh,' Cathy said, 'I meant the...'

The other doctor laughed. 'Of course.'

Finally, she gave her it. It was only the aripiprazole, but she was glad of even that now.

'And if you have any joint problems while you're here, just come in and we'll...'

But Cathy had already opened the door. 'Many thanks,' she said cheerily and left.

Standing outside the practice, she finally gave way. Tears streamed down her cheeks and she hurriedly began to walk, blotting at her face with her sleeves. Oh God, how awful. How excruciating. If she ever, even accidentally, met Dr Cosgrove again, she'd die. What had she been thinking of trying to trick another doctor into prescribing her opiates? What had she turned into? An addict, she had joked, but that was what she fundamentally was. An addict and a liar.

15

The old doctor had been unable to settle to anything despite it being a busy Monday morning. Even a rather odd request from a temporary resident hadn't distracted her for long. She had been feeling edgy since the church service. On Sunday night, she hadn't slept particularly well and had ended up coming down to her writing desk, in an attempt to do some work. Sometimes she did this, even in the middle of the night.

Despite being close to retirement, Dr Cosgrove took the responsibility of her work extremely seriously, particularly keeping up-to-date with the latest advances in medicine. She had always done so, even as a single-GP partner at the beginning. Especially then, in fact. She knew only too well that with no other GPs around, it might be easy to get lazy in her prescribing habits, using the same old favourites and not moving with the times. Her father had warned her of this. He had seen her mother change from a confident, independent practitioner to a fearful one, simply because she had lost touch with modern medicine. Terrified of making a mistake, missing a diagnosis. It was a slippery slope. If a doctor wasn't confident, how could they expect their patients to believe in what they said?

It had been rare in those days for a woman to choose a career in medicine, although not unheard of by any means. Dr Cosgrove knew her mother had been highly intelligent. But with that, came a weakness also. Looking back now, Dr Cosgrove could see her mother had probably been afraid for the majority of her working life. A perfectionist. It must have been an immense strain. Dr Cosgrove could remember the hushed conversations. Her mother's voice, high-pitched and imploring, her father's, reassuring but firm. There had been mistakes, she knew that much from listening on the stairs. She had sat in her nightdress, huddled on the staircase, resting her forehead against the cold wood of the banisters as they spoke.

She hated secrets. Her father and she were usually a team, as she saw it. They had little understandings, not quite jokes, but familiarities. Her mother had always been a bit of an outsider in that respect. That had all changed when her mother had stopped work. It was never explained to her as a child, but she supposed now it was some form of neurotic anxiety or depression. Her father hadn't had as much time to spend with her and, rather than sit and talk when he returned from work, he would run heavily up the stairs to see her mother, who had taken to her bedroom throughout the day.

She did return to work eventually, but things had changed. The conversation over the dinner table was now dominated by her mother reciting her difficult cases supposedly to entertain them, but the guise was veiled thinly. At the end of each case description, her mother would look sideways at her father, as if to check for approval. Her father didn't look up from his plate and often turned the conversation to something more neutral. Heather rarely spoke at the dinner table anymore, feeling very distant from both of her parents at this time. Her father became older and more tired.

Dr Cosgrove shook her head. And what would her parents think if they knew about her troubles now? She got up from her desk and crossed the room. Another letter had arrived while she had been out taking her stroll yesterday evening. Now, no longer bothering to enjoy the anonymity of the postal service, the deliverer had chanced being seen and slipped the letter through her door. Perhaps they now wished to be known. What if she had seen them? What would she have done? The letter had been a horrible shock, and so unfair. Sunday was meant to be a safe day. She had been wholly unprepared. This time, the meaning was unmistakable.

On Monday morning, fatigued from lack of sleep, she had arrived at her beloved practice to find that she was duty doctor for the day. This meant that all the non-routine appointment requests and house-visits would come to her. It was an element of the profession that she disliked, not allowing her the ability to plan and prioritise time. All that morning, she felt that something dreadful might be around the corner.

She saw little of her colleagues, taking telephone consultations almost as soon as she arrived. Ruth, she had spotted in the distance twice. She had hoped her partner might go out of her way to touch base and apologise for her behaviour on the Friday before, but it seemed that she would have to wait. Perhaps none of it mattered anymore. A dreadful inevitability hung in the air.

By early lunchtime, things had become quieter. She had ten minutes before the next patient, having been gifted a non-attender. She felt somehow detached looking at herself in the long mirror mounted on her wall. Like a casual on-looker critiquing the appearance of an unsuspecting passer-by through a window. For a moment, she studied the lines along her forehead and around her eyes, wondering if she knew herself at all. When had she become old? Even her mother, submerged by the heavy pull of Alzheimer's, had still looked younger than she did right now. But she had never had her mother's features. Instead of a petite, delicate nose and cheekbones, she had inherited her father's stubborn jaw. She jutted it out further and saw her father who had been surprisingly inattentive this last day or so.

Since the church service, she had spoken to him, but he had failed to answer.

'Where have you been?' she asked him.

His reflection was clear in the mirror and gazed back.

'I've been needing you. Why didn't you come to the house instead of here? You know I can't talk properly during a surgery.'

Her father placed a hand on her right shoulder. A firm, reassuring touch.

'I'm frightened, Father. Don't you know what's been going on? Everything's wrong.'

He nodded. Still, his hand rested on her.

'Why won't you speak?' she shouted suddenly, shrugging herself free of him and picking the nearest thing to hand, which happened to be her stethoscope. She hurled it at the mirror. It landed with a splintering crack.

She was perfectly composed for her next patient. No one would have seen the involuntary muscle spasm in her cheek as she printed out the prescription. Nor would they have noticed, as she walked to the door to guide the patient from her room, the patch of psoriasis on her calf, always a telltale sign that she was overworked and stressed. Even the crack to the bottom right corner of her mirror went unseen.

When one of the receptionists knocked on her door to query a referral letter she had dictated, Dr Cosgrove was fully recovered from the silly upset earlier. Just a wobble. She must take home that steroid cream for her leg.

'A shout from my room?' Dr Cosgrove asked when questioned. 'Oh? No, no, that was nothing. I just dropped something on my foot.' She laughed. The lie came easily. 'How has it been, out the front? All quiet now?' The girl said that it was quite manageable now. 'Good, good,' she replied. 'Has Dr Davage gone out again? Oh, she has. No, nothing urgent at all. It can wait.'

When the girl left, Dr Cosgrove rested back in her chair and sighed.

She eventually spoke to Ruth that afternoon. Her partner seemed surprised by how upset she had been over the quarrel on Friday. She denied avoiding Dr Cosgrove that day and said that it had been too hectic to catch up earlier. Dr Cosgrove was not satisfied. She hadn't failed to see Ruth's raised eyebrows and how she had glanced away in distaste when she had mentioned the retirement again.

Throughout the conversation with her partner, Dr Cosgrove wanted to tell her about the dreadful letters. But when she left Ruth's room, again without confiding, she knew that the opportunity had passed and she must proceed alone. In many ways, the decision brought with it some peace. An acceptance that she had been searching for, for so long.

She did not usually take her walks during the week, preferring to enjoy this solitary exercise when she had more time and energy. Typically, this meant on weekends or days off. Today, however, was different.

By the time Dr Cosgrove completed the circuit of Kinnaven, turning from the dank heather-clad clifftops to make her journey home, she had made her decision and knew what she must do.

16

When Dr Cosgrove had been established in Kinnaven for several years, her relationship with her parents had matured to some extent. Her father, now fully occupied with her quietly dementing mother, no longer had time to offer advice concerning the day-to-day running of the surgery. At first, Dr Cosgrove had relied on him heavily, finding that she had no confidence in her own judgement. When he showed less of an interest, she had been fretful. She had tested his devotion during the less regular visits or telephone calls, finding herself fractious and inpatient, almost goading him into a disagreement. Afterwards, she regretted her behaviour terribly.

As time went on, however, and as her status as a doctor began to be accepted in the small town, she depended on him less. Word got around that she was a highly competent and diligent doctor and her patients' trust confirmed for her that she had made the right choice in coming to the village. She had always been a determined individual and she felt it her duty to serve what she now saw as her community for the rest of her working days, and to the very best of her ability.

Nowadays, young doctors came and went. The locums, for

example. They were off to a new job before you even knew they had been in the building. That was not the kind of life for her. She saw herself as being at the heart of the village, and although she detached herself from the people emotionally, choosing to have no social interactions with her patients, she still felt a kinship with those she served. She would not leave Kinnaven. Not ever. With this decision, came a new sense of calm. She had always seen things through to the end and this was no different.

Dr Cosgrove returned from her walk, flushed and content. For the first time in months, she felt at peace. She hung up her jacket and slowly walked through to the living room, looking at her beloved paintings as she went, smiling at the shine on the banisters and momentarily paused to stroke the polished wood. She checked the answer machine, finding that the red light was flashing intermittently signalling a missed call. It was Ruth. She listened to her message. Just a query regarding something they had discussed earlier in the day. Ruth had wanted to say more to her before she left but hadn't managed. It didn't matter. She trusted Ruth to take care of things.

Following an enjoyable meal of scrambled eggs, Dr Cosgrove settled herself comfortably in her favourite chair. She had put the lamps on and drawn the curtains, giving the room a warm buttery glow. She poured herself a small glass of port. It was one she had been saving for a special occasion and she felt that this evening was just such a time. Any concern of the day was now gone. Nothing troubled her now.

By her armchair was her doctors' bag. It was a Gladstone given to her by her father. She felt it important. It must come with her. She knew others would do things differently. The doctors' bag contained an array of options. But she was old-school and always had been. Dr Cosgrove was never one to shirk her responsibilities. She checked the time. Yes. She must prepare. Her shoes would be dry now, and her jacket would be warm having been rested on the heater in the hall. Ignoring her father's protestations, she unclipped the door latch and lifting the hood of her coat, went out into the rain.

As dusk settled on the town of Kinnaven, enveloping it in a gentle mat of darkness, doves cooed softly to one another, finding the best place to roost. The port had warmed her, and settling into a familiar rhythm, Dr Cosgrove took her usual path. She had passed this way so many times before. She could do it in her sleep. Forgetting the rain, she turned her head skywards, allowing its cool, damp touch. In her hand, she still held her doctors' bag. She had always loved a neat ending.

The doves were silent now, nesting up by the church. Making her final walk of the day, the upright figure, flanked by an elderly man and a woman, passed them by. Her face was a beacon of happiness now she had finally come home.

17

Cathy woke at four. Unable to sleep any longer, she went out. She had no reason to do so, but it didn't matter. It had rained heavily earlier and the ground was wet beneath her feet. As she moved through the garden, guided only by the light from the moon, she barely knew what she was doing. It was like sleepwalking, and perhaps it was best that way. A self-protective mechanism. The gate opened with a squeal. The hinges needing oiling. Cathy paused and listened, her fingers glancing at the bubbled paint on metal. Now, all she heard was the booming of the sea. It called to her.

Don't hesitate, she told herself. Just move. Keep moving forward. She plunged off-road, her boots barely protecting her legs from the wet grasses that slapped as she stumbled and slipped. She skirted the edge of the field, avoiding the farmer's crop. Initially, she was afraid, but the further she went, the more she felt like running. That's what she wanted more than anything: to run until her heart burst from her chest.

Her pace quickened. The field ended, and she was out on the moor. The heathery scrubland was coarse and the vegetation dense. She followed some kind of a path, tripping and jogging as she went. Something shone in the moonlight by her feet, a reflection in the undergrowth. Cathy leapt in fear, not knowing what it was. But she continued, determined not to be distracted from her cause. The path was obvious and bare at times from previous walkers, but in some places, she had to guess. Her destination remained unchanged though, and with this motivation, she moved. Her feet took her there. The sea had called to her, and she had come.

There, she stood for what seemed like an eternity, looking out upon endless grey water. So vast that she couldn't help but be in awe. She didn't look down at the rocks. Instead, she breathed deeply. In and out. The cold, early-morning air chilled her. She wondered how it would feel. She had rehearsed it a thousand times in her dreams. The first step would be the hardest. There would be air and wind. And then, nothing. Above all, she feared the noise. She again recalled the crazed laughter of her nightmares and prayed that it would not be so. Instead, she focused on the music once more. Since she had become more erratic in taking her prescribed tablets, it had returned.

As she stood there, she considered all the patients she had tried to help throughout her career. Some had expressed a wish to die. She had listened with sympathy but she could not say that she had understood. They had spoken of a resolution. Those were the really serious ones. The ones who had made up their minds for sure. They said that there was a sudden inner calm. Indecision: that was the worst of it.

But Cathy had found no peace and she no longer recognised herself. She had turned into something she did not want to be. Her vocation was at an end. Even if she did return to work, she would have to be monitored and watched. Every movement, every mood swing would have ramifications.

And then there was the rest. The worst of it. She had made

promises to her partners, and Suzalinna. She had turned herself into a liar. She had not hesitated in deceiving them. It had been so easy. Had she always been this way, even before she was ill? Such hypocrisy. What did her CV say? 'Special interest in addiction psychiatry and substance misuse'. What a joke that was now. 'I'm clean,' she had told the psychiatrist before she left, and he had believed her. The opiates had been too easy to steal. Every doctor had access to them in one form or another. Cathy's practice kept their controlled drugs in a locked store cupboard. They had a logbook to sign. But it had been simple to do. She had the bloody key on her keyring now. Too easy.

Hot tears stung at her eyes. She had cried so much that night that the creases of skin were raw and inflamed. The morphine hadn't worked for more than an hour or so, and she knew she'd have to take another tablet if she was to sleep. What had she done? She rubbed at her face, enjoying the discomfort of the abrasive material of her skin. Blinking, she stepped closer. She had to be able to see as she did this. She would not be a coward. She had to face it with her eyes open.

She shuffled to the edge. The wind had picked up and whipped her hair across her face. She looked down at the rocks directly below. The white spume from the waves rushed in, crashing high up the cliff face. The rocks themselves were near-black and shone in the half-light, glistening and harsh. This torment would be over soon enough. One last act of bravery, to atone for all of her faults. She inhaled slow and deep, filling her lungs with icy-breeze. One last breath and then...

For some reason, Cathy glanced to the side before taking her final step. What she saw was incomprehensible. To the left of the huge rock that came almost to the height of the cliff face itself, lay something dreadful. And despite the distance, Cathy recognised what it was immediately.

18

News of the doctor's death did not take long to travel along the streets of Kinnaven. It spread like the tide, rearing its head in a great wave and crashing down upon the residents, spreading fast and without mercy on all that it met.

Full of concern, Jean was at Cathy's door by nine o'clock that morning. She had been due to clean at the farmhouse anyway but Alison had sent her down having already heard the gossip herself.

'My God!' Jean said, having swept into the cottage disregarding the formality of invitation. 'Dead! But I still don't understand what you were doing out there in the middle of the night.'

Cathy gulped the tea that Jean had made and pulled the blanket that she had also insisted upon, around her shoulders a little tighter.

The police had said they would come later in the morning to interview her. They had been so kind and had not made things any worse for her than necessary. Both Iain and Alison had been sympathetic too, suggesting she come up to the farmhouse to stay, but she had wanted to be alone. For a time, there had been nothing but noise and more than anything Cathy wished to escape the sirens and the shouts. It was almost as if her mind couldn't stand anymore.

Some dreadful hours had passed while she waited for the sun to properly rise. Cathy had hardly known what to do with herself. Initially, she stood with her hands clasped tightly, watching at the window as swarms of police officers descended the craggy coastline, a beautiful backdrop for such a tragic event. When she observed two helmeted men in bright orange jumpsuits arrive, carrying between them an empty stretcher, she stepped away from the window and refused to watch anymore. Instead, she moved through the house and sat in the kitchen at the back, hearing muffled calls and the engines of cars as they arrived or departed from the scene. That was how Jean had found her, sitting on a kitchen stool alone, cold and shaking, still wearing her boots and pyjamas.

Jean's voice came to her once more, as if from a great distance, and Cathy had to actively force herself back to the present.

'I've no idea what she had been thinking,' Jean said, as much to herself as to Cathy. 'You know, I had a feeling something was odd when I woke up this morning. There was something not right. I'd never have thought it of her though, but old Mrs Spratt said as much to me once. Something about resilience, I think. Well anyway, it's a shame for her and for all those who have to deal with what she did. Some people might call it selfish. They already are. Doing something like that and to hell with the consequences. Goodness knows what my mother'll have to say about it, but she's never been that keen on the old doctor, anyway.' Jean sighed. 'And I was in only yesterday, cleaning. You'd have thought I'd have got a feeling. It's not as if I'm psychic or anything,' Jean quickly reassured her. 'Honestly, though, I can't believe she did it.'

Cathy had tasted the tea she was drinking and spluttered, suddenly noticing the sickly sweetness of the liquid.

'You're looking better,' Jean remarked. 'Getting a bit more colour to your cheeks now. What a terrible shock it must have been for you. See, the old doctor didn't think about that, did she? Someone had to find her and you were the unlucky one.'

Cathy nodded.

'Well, come on then,' Jean said. 'Why were you out in the middle of the night wandering the cliffs? You must have been catching your death out there.'

'I had a nightmare,' she answered mechanically, but her face must have paled and perhaps Jean saw her hand tighten on the mug so that the knuckles showed white.

'Well, it turned into a real nightmare, looking down and seeing that! God knows, what a horror.' Jean, possibly realising the insensitivity of her words, patted Cathy on the arm. 'I'm sorry,' she said. 'Such a horrible thing for you.'

Cathy smiled for the first time. She and Jean knew little of one another and here was this other woman, her cleaner, and perhaps five or ten years her junior, comforting her. Cathy's heart warmed to her now, seeing Jean's chatter for what it was: straightforward interest and no pretence. Jean might well have tiptoed around the cottage, speaking in hushed tones, but instead, she seemed more comfortable with the idea of sudden death than perhaps she was herself. Just having Jean there lifted the mood of the place, which made Cathy feel more human again. Repeatedly, Jean said that she should have known something was wrong with the doctor and couldn't understand why she had not.

'I think I should shower before the police come. They said they'd be up later,' Cathy said, getting up more steadily now. 'You don't have to stay, you know. I'm fine.'

As she flicked on the fan for the bathroom, she paused. In

the next room, she could hear Jean talking. 'Might not have sensed it about her, but I did about you,' Jean said thoughtfully. Cathy pretended that she hadn't heard.

Once showered, she felt better and more like herself. Jean had made two slices of toast and was reloading the toaster.

'Funny how a shock makes you hungry, isn't it?' Jean said in explanation. 'Jam? I think you should.'

While they sat in the kitchen with their second mug of tea and, Cathy thought, her fourth slice of toast, the police arrived. She had dealt with the police on multiple occasions with work and had even been called to court as an expert witness after examining a patient who had been assaulted by her husband. She knew the drill and answered the two officers as best she could, taking her time so her words could be written down, and then repeating any areas that didn't immediately make sense. But there was little she could tell them other than what they knew already. She had been out walking early and had, by chance, looked down and seen the doctor lying there at the base of the cliffs. They asked if she had seen anything at the top of the cliffs, or any sign that the doctor might have passed that way. Cathy shook her head. They asked if she had seen anyone else when she was out walking but, again, Cathy had nothing to add.

As they got up to leave, the older constable snapped his notebook shut and sighed. 'Such a waste,' he said. 'All that intelligence and she threw it away, and nearing retirement, so they say.'

Jean, who had been hovering indiscreetly in the kitchen doorway, finally spoke. 'Jim, did they find a note?'

The older officer turned. 'Jean Scott, you know I can't answer that,' he said severely.

'You'll be wanting to question me next, I suppose?'

'And why would we want to do that?' he asked, zipping up his jacket and moving towards the door.

'Well, I cleaned for her. Maybe you'll want me to let you into the house and see if anything's been moved. Only yesterday I was in there.'

The policeman laughed. 'I think we have that all in hand, Jean, but thanks all the same.'

Jean looked disappointed.

The policeman turned once more to Cathy. 'You'll be hearing from us, of course. Until things are firmed up, I'd ask for you to stay in the area, if that's convenient? Take care of yourself. It looks like you have a fine devotee here anyway.' He looked across again at Jean and smiled.

It took Cathy almost the entire afternoon to convince Jean that she was really all right to be left. After she had gone, Cathy moved about the cottage, deep in thought. With Jean there, she had been preoccupied with the simple, reassuring babble of her new-found friend, but now that she was alone, her thoughts repeatedly returned to the image of the doctor lying there. The twist of her legs, the unnatural angle of her head and neck, the pallor of the woman's face and the blood.

Aimlessly, she touched the cushions on the sofa and folded and refolded a jumper. She had met Dr Cosgrove only last week. Maybe she ought to have noticed something herself. She had been too distracted with her own issues, of course. Jean had thought that as the doctor's cleaner, she should have known, but she, Cathy, might have recognised it with her medical training. Cathy replayed their meeting. It had been excruciating for her, but had the old doctor showed anything to suggest her suicidal ideation? Could there have been an indication of low mood? But as she mentally ran through the difficult conversation: Dr Cosgrove's genuine interest in her recent diagnosis and her kind but frank dialogue when she had requested the opiates, Cathy knew that this was an absurd line of thought. Having only met the woman once, how on earth could she make a judgement on the other doctor's mental health? In hindsight, it seemed ridiculous to think they had been sitting talking about Cathy's state of mind, when in fact, perhaps Dr Cosgrove should have been speaking about her own.

Cathy wondered if she had found some peace before she made her decision to die. She certainly hoped so. But what had forced her to choose such a violent end? Having met the woman, Cathy did feel somehow compelled to find out why. Suicide was always shocking, but when it was a doctor, a member of your own profession, it seemed especially so. Doctors were meant to be immune to mental illness. She had come so close. One more step. Had the sea called that night to Dr Cosgrove too?

19

'Look, darling,' he said. His voice, so smooth and caressing, pierced her heart like a knife. 'You know we've not done anything wrong. This doesn't change a thing. Don't go losing your head just because some old doctor killed herself.'

Jean shot him a look.

'I know, I'm sorry if it sounds brutal but surely you can see it doesn't change our plans? I'm sorry the old dear chucked herself over, really, I am. The place is called Devil's Leap for a reason, isn't it? She probably had some incurable illness or something of the sort and took the quickest way out. And who could blame her for that?' Ross pulled her to him and held her head tightly against his chest. 'Sweet Jean, I do love you even when you get angry but don't go messing things up now when we're just beginning.'

Jean removed herself from his embrace. 'There are police crawling all over the place, Ross. Are you completely mad? How can we? Are you honestly suggesting we start scouting out houses now? What's the rush anyway? Why can't we wait? While there are so many odd people in the village, we're asking for trouble.'

Ross walked to the window and turned his back to her. She could see his shoulder drop and him shaking his head. Her heart sank.

'Oh God, don't.' She wasn't sure how much more she could take.

Ross turned to face her again. He blinked, and a tear rolled down his cheek. Rather than wipe it, he allowed it to travel downwards, lingering on the point of his cheekbone and then finally dropping to the floor. 'He's been back in touch again,' he whispered. 'We need to get that money.'

'Oh, Ross, you're scaring me now! Can't you explain to this man that we'll pay him back, but in instalments?'

Ross looked at her savagely. For a moment, she thought he was going to hit her and she recoiled. 'Don't you understand?' he spat. 'These people are not the sort to negotiate with. We need the money and we need it fast. If you care anything about me, you'll help me. If not, it's time to get out. But God have mercy on you because if I don't sort this, it'll be me at the bottom of those cliffs before the week is through.'

'For God's sake! I never said I wanted that.' She began to cry. Sobs wracked through her, but he didn't reach out to comfort her. She gulped and slowed her breathing. Wiping her face with her sleeve, she looked at him. 'All right,' she nodded, 'tell me what I need to do.'

He kissed her forehead and told her how good she was. She was better than him. She was kind and honest, and he hated asking for help. If only there had been another way. But once the money was paid, he would give her the life that she and Calum deserved. He would always be grateful.

Although not unmoved by this speech, Jean found the sentiment wearing thin.

'This one's risky, for the very reason you've said,' he began. 'But it's a risk worth taking simply because I think it's our best chance to get a lot in one go, and that means we'd not have to put ourselves at such jeopardy again. I don't see the point in slipping a fiver here or there from Mrs Hutchison's purse or the minister's collection. If we do this, it'll buy us some breathing space.'

She was almost afraid to ask.

'The doctor,' Ross said.

'What, down at the holiday lets? Oh please, no. I like her. I get the feeling she's not well. It seems unfair.'

Ross held up a hand. 'Not her. We'll not get anything from there. I've already been in and she hasn't got a thing. No, the other doctor. Old Dr Cosgrove. That's where we need to be. Don't look so horrified, Jean. You've already stolen from one dead old lady, so I don't see how this is any different. And you still have the keys to the house.'

Jean recoiled in horror. 'Ross, but the police! We'd be seen going through the house looking for things and what would we take anyway?'

'Don't be like that,' he said testily. 'I'm no fool. It's not like we're going to walk in in broad daylight and start raking through her stuff. God, what do you take me for? I wish we'd optimised our situation with Mrs Spratt. How much more money could we have taken from her cupboard if we'd only had the head for it? I'm not going to make that mistake again. Dr Cosgrove had no close relatives by the sounds of things so, with few visitors to the house, nothing will be missed. An ornament here or there, perhaps jewellery. Of course, I'm hoping we'll find cash. That would be ideal. This is what I had hoped to do anyway, but more gradually while she was alive. It would have been fine if you had slipped something in your pocket when you were in cleaning last week, at least then it might have got us started. Anyway, this new development simply means we have to be more thorough and get in and out without being seen.'

As he spoke, something in her shifted. Jean had always been an independent sort of a person. She was resourceful and clever. She had had to be over the years and only more so since Daniel had left. Now that she had promised Ross she'd help, she swallowed down any further protest. *Just get the thing done and over with*, she told herself. That was the only way. Inwardly, she pushed her doubts to the back of her mind. It might all turn out for the best anyway.

She was surprised that over the following day, her reaction changed further. Of course, she was still torn by what they planned to do, but with that came a wave of something new. Perhaps it was excitement. The idea of her and Ross accomplishing something together. Coming out the other side, adrenaline-filled and exhilarated. She was giddy with excitement. Imagine if they pulled it off. Ross would be so grateful and relieved to put his troubles behind him. She would feel wonderful having helped him through his darkest time. And, of course, eventually, good things would come their way. If Ross's father died, and surely that couldn't be so far in the future, they would live comfortably together; the three of them. Perhaps they'd move away from Kinnaven entirely. It seemed sensible to make a fresh start. Calum would make new friends and go to a better school, gaining the opportunities that neither she nor Ross had had. They might choose a cottage in the country. Buy it outright and Ross could spend his weekends doing it up while she did the garden. Her mother would come to visit regularly and would be so proud that she had found this happiness after all of her troubles in the past.

'So then,' Jean said, now quite matter-of-fact. 'What's your plan and when do we begin?'

They spent an hour before Calum came home from school, discussing the scheme. At first, she was dismayed to hear that she was to go alone, but as Ross said, it did make more sense for only one of them to go and she was by far the better of the two, knowing the layout of the house already. They discussed the details at length, even shortlisting the likely places she should look. Ross finally went through his emergency, worst-case scenario, strategy. If disturbed, she should get out the back bathroom window and return to the house via the steps behind the church, rather than the road. If worst came to worst and she was caught, she might easily explain that she was the cleaner and had panicked when the doctor had died, having left her watch at the house, but had then been afraid to say anything to the police. As long as she kept her head though, nothing of the sort should have to come into play. Minimal noise or light as she moved around the house, and cleverness about what she took. That was the key to the scheme's success.

The idea seemed so simple during the afternoon but as the hours had passed, Jean became more and more anxious. It was to happen that night, he said. It was hard to stay rational once the decision was made. Jean was distracted and bad-tempered. She shouted at Calum and sent him up to bed early, regretting it almost as soon as it was done. Ross arrived back, having been to the farmhouse, saying he needed to check on his brother or something. He was sitting in the living room now watching the television and trying to keep things as ordinary for her as possible. He had already thanked her a thousand times and promised to make it up to her, but probably seeing her increasing edginess, he had left her to her own devices. He would be there for her when she came home. She had to force herself to think of that.

Opening the living room door, she looked in. Ross went to get up.

'Don't bother,' she told him.

She refused to kiss him. She couldn't bring herself to be touched. And so, she crept through to the hallway, hoping not to disturb Calum, and slipped on her jacket. As she left, she felt in her pocket and allowed her fingers to encircle the cold metal of the key to Dr Cosgrove's house.

All the way, she held the key between her thumb and forefinger inside her jacket pocket, her head down. She didn't meet a soul, only being startled once by a cat as it suddenly darted out from behind a hedge. She arrived far faster than she had expected, or perhaps, wanted. The house reared up in front of her in the darkness. As she unlocked the front door, quickly checking around that no one was observing, her heart pounded so loudly that she felt she might either faint or be sick. *Stop being stupid*, she told herself. *You've got this far already. There is no turning back.* The house was in complete darkness. Fumbling to remove the key from the lock, she gently closed the door behind her and stood listening in the hallway. It was cold, almost unnaturally so. A shiver ran through her and she wrapped the folds of her jacket around herself. She didn't have long and she knew what she must do first. Reaching into her pocket, she fished out her mobile phone and switched it on. Just as Ross had said, it would allow a small amount of light to guide her through the house.

The light cast a jerky shroud of shadows around the hallway as she crept on. She tried to focus but it took a minute or so for her eyes to adjust. When they did so, she felt more confident to move on through the hall. She ran up the stairs, cringing as the fourth step creaked. She paused a moment and then continued. The doctor's bedroom was where she headed first. Ross had assumed that it was the place where the jewellery and any precious mementoes would be kept. Jean had already seen the dressing table and, although she had not been asked to do the room, she had popped her head in and had spotted that the doctor had some pretty earrings.

She had brought a leather handbag. A medium to large size

that had once belonged to her mother but had been passed to her when she had tired of the thing. Jean hadn't used it before, thinking the style old-fashioned, but it fitted the purpose that day, being a reasonable size and the zip to the main compartment could be moved easily without noise. Anyone passing her in the street would think nothing of seeing her carrying it.

Having selected not all but a good number of the doctor's trinkets and charms, including what looked like diamond earrings with a matching necklace, an expensive-looking watch and a set of pearl beads, Jean closed the bag and shut the drawer. She glanced around to make sure nothing looked disturbed. She then retraced her steps downstairs.

For some reason, the living room gave her more concern. Perhaps it was because the bedroom had been slightly impersonal as if any middle-aged woman might have stayed there. The downstairs of the house, on the other hand, was clearly where the doctor had spent the majority of her time. Jean became jumpier and twice switched off her phone and froze in silence, fearing that she had heard a noise outside. On both occasions, she was forced to go on, knowing that the real treasure might be found here.

The police had left little trace of their interference, although she knew they must have had a look around, if not least, for a suicide note. She crossed the room to the writing bureau. This was the part she had been fearing the most. It was undoubtedly where the doctor kept her paperwork. Jean wasn't superstitious but like many women who, for generations, had lived on that rough Scottish coastline, she got 'feelings' about things. Some might call it psychic, but Jean did not. She was more level-headed than that. It was a part of herself that she tried hard to repress, fearing that it would give her the jitters if she allowed it. All the same, the last time she had cleaned here, she had felt something about that room. There was something within the bureau that was causing her to feel it even now. The sensation grew in intensity as she lifted the lid. Trying to remain calm, she guided the top down to its resting position. She placed her mobile phone carefully down to give her further light and deftly flicked through the doctor's papers. Here, as Ross had hoped, she found an envelope full of cash. She had no time to count it, but estimated that there was about a hundred. The bag was on the armchair beside her. She slid the money in beside the jewellery.

Against all of her inclination, she then drew out the central drawer and pressed her fingers together to squeeze into the compartment that she knew was there. Her grandparents had owned a writing desk just like this. She still remembered her granddad showing her the secret drawer. If the police had looked in here hoping to find a suicide note, they had missed the hidden drawer, because it came out stiffly. The wood stuck and then came suddenly free. She touched the edge of what must be paper and immediately pulled back. It was as if she had been burnt. Taking a deep breath, she steadied herself, planting her feet squarely on the ground and almost feeling for the earth far beneath her. Once more, she reached in and touched the paper. This time, she managed to withdraw her finger and thumb while tightly clenching what appeared to be a crumpled letter.

The light on her mobile phone went out, but undeterred, Jean fumbled and found the switch. Waves of revulsion swept over her. She felt the hairs on the back of her neck rise and although she fought to go on, she couldn't block it out. Her hands were now shaking so much that closing the desk was, in itself, a difficult task. She hastily composed herself before placing the letter not in the bag with the rest of the doctor's possessions, but in her jacket pocket. Why she did this, she could not say, but it seemed important. She then fled the house.

The rain had come on again. It felt refreshing, almost cleansing, on her skin. The gradient of the hill grew steeper and she slowed to a walk, head bowed but ploughing on, only focused on the line of water that tracked down the hill and along the gutter. The sound of water hitting the drain as she passed gave her some comfort, a gurgling, almost tuneful reassurance that she was nearly home.

She wouldn't allow herself to think about what she had just done. Not until she was home with the door closed. Once inside, she would make herself a cup of tea and creep upstairs to check on Calum. Just as long as he hadn't missed her. She didn't feel like she could face Ross. She prayed he would realise and not make a fuss.

He was waiting for her, of course. He took her jacket, guided her through to the kitchen and shut the door. The kettle was boiled, but he offered her wine or a shot of something, whatever she wanted. He had slipped the bag from her shoulder as she had come in. It sat on the worktop. Jean couldn't look at the damn thing, but he unzipped it and peered inside.

'Well, well, well,' he said, looking up at her and smiling. 'The girl's done good.'

Jean promptly spun around, only making it just in time to vomit in the kitchen sink.

20

With her eyes closed, Cathy stood listening. Far below, she heard the rhythmical swish of tidewater as it played on shingle. Down and to the left, the occasional thundering boom, as a larger wave hit the rocks that encircled the small cove. The last time she had been here, she had come so close but so much had changed since then. It had only been that morning, but it felt like a lifetime ago.

She sighed and reached into her pocket. It seemed right that she should do it now. Who was she kidding hiding them at the bottom of her bag anyway? If there was temptation, she would slip up again. She took the foil packet. Only two tablets of diamorphine left. She had counted them many times over in her mind. A backup just in case, taken from her medical practice. Stolen to all effects, for her personal use. But she didn't feel the need for backups any longer. The old doctor's death had shown her the fragility of life. She owed it to herself, owed it to her patients if she was to ever serve them again.

With a flick, they were gone, tossed into the breeze. The packet snatched and tumbled, somersaulting down into the lathered sea below. Twice, it caught the light and glinted at her.

And suddenly, she recalled the glint of something else in the heather the last time she had been here. She wondered if it had been a flight of fancy, but turning from the clifftops, she slowly retraced her steps from that early morning when she had stumbled half-blind with tears and self-loathing.

She searched for a good ten minutes until she found it. Again, it was the light falling on metal that gave it away. She stooped and examined the silver disc, holding it in her palm. She wondered when it had been dropped. She didn't understand why, but she knew that she couldn't return it to its owner just yet. Instead, she slipped it into her pocket and continued on her way. The breeze caught her hair and whipped the loose strands across her face.

A couple of gulls screamed overhead, and looking skywards, Cathy followed their path as they swooped in an arc, calling indignantly to one another. As she watched the birds' flight, she saw, for the first time, a figure to the far left of her further along the cliffs. Was it the lone watcher from before? The person was too far away to distinguish, and she couldn't tell if it was a man or a woman. Whoever it was, was sitting this time. Then she realised that the rectangle obscuring half of the figure was, in fact, a board and that it must be an artist at work.

She paused for a moment, unsure whether to approach. Then she picked her way slowly across the heathery wasteland. As she grew closer, she saw the figure was that of a thin, elderly man seated in a canvas folding chair. Prepared for the extreme weather, he had covered his nose and mouth with a scarf. On his head, he wore a tweed cap, allowing Cathy only a glimpse of piercing blue eyes and a ruddy nose. On his lap was a tartan blanket which he had wrapped around his legs, presumably anticipating a long afternoon sketching.

'Hello,' Cathy called as she approached, and for a moment she wondered if the man was going to ignore her. She had come towards him at an angle, but she would have been impossible to miss. He had looked past her, almost pointedly avoiding communication. But now, he placed his brush down and turned his attention to her.

'Yes,' he replied through the scarf and, perhaps realising how inaudible the interaction would be, lowered it to show a slightly mocking, thin pair of lips.

'Cold day to be painting,' she said.

'It is.'

He had a mildly sardonic tone that made her feel uncomfortable. Cathy pushed her hands deep into her pockets.

'Strangely,' he continued, 'I find that unless urged on in some way, be it through discomfort, cold or whatever, I never really seem to do my work justice. Rather as if the insistence to finish gives my brushwork the same resolve and dynamism that I am feeling.'

He smiled vaguely at this concept, although Cathy felt sure that this was more to himself than to her. It was as if she was overhearing a private joke. She glanced around, wondering how on earth the man had found his way to such a desolate spot. There was no path or road, but perhaps being a local, he knew the area far better than she. She was sure she had not passed him on the way to the cliffs.

'Not one of my best,' he said, gesturing to the painting. 'I'm afraid. I can tell within the first few brushstrokes how it feels, and this one feels distinctly mediocre. Although, it's a matter of taste. People will buy anything if they see something in a painting that relates to them. Sometimes, I feel like a go-between. Supply and demand.'

Cathy came around to stand beside him and was struck by the ferocity of the seascape. She was almost at a loss for words. The man looked up at her.

'Bit wild for you, is it? I'm not to everyone's taste.'

'No, no really. It's so powerful.'

The man had obviously heard praise of this sort before. She could see that she was losing him. His paint-daubed hand was already reaching for a cloth, and his focus was no longer on her but on something, some catch in the light or shadow he had yet to capture. Cathy noticed the nicotine-stained forefinger with clubbing of his fingernails. From a professional point of view, she wondered if he knew he was unwell. But it was none of her business.

'I'm Cathy, by the way. I think I've seen your work in a gallery in the next town perhaps. Do you live nearby?'

This comment only seemed to further deepen the man's disinterest in her. He grunted and waved a bony hand in the direction further along the cliffs. Cathy saw for the first time a small, ramshackle cottage pressed against the rise in the moors. How she could have missed it, she did not know. What a lonely life but it was probably how he liked it. Just him and his paintings. The man had picked up his paintbrush and was gazing out to sea. Deciding that she had been dismissed, Cathy moved away feeling angry at her loss for words. How odd to be painting on such a day. Had he not heard of the tragedy that morning?

Incensed, the gulls circled overhead. She flinched at their deafening screeches. Perhaps they had been guarding the artist all the while and her company had been not only unwanted by the man, but by them as well.

By the time she had made her way back to the cottage, she decided that if she did come across the man again, she would steer well clear.

21

The note was brief. Jean read and reread it, unsure what to make of the thing. So old Dr Cosgrove had left a message after all. What a thing to find. But the contents, rather than explaining her decision, only confused things further. It was almost an obituary, Jean thought, but even for that, it was too sparse. She cast her mind back to Mrs Spratt's notice in the local paper. It too had been simple but had at least mention of the old lady's life, her love for her husband and son, and her contentment at ending her days in the village she had much admired. If Dr Cosgrove had intended on this being some kind of a similar epilogue, she had fallen far short of the mark. Refolding the paper, Jean replaced it in the back of her bathroom cabinet. It was ridiculous to feel this way really, but she wanted to keep it to herself. Ross had already disappeared to Aberdeen with the rest of the spoils, hoping to pawn them. The note, she decided, was hers alone. A memento of the doctor and a reminder of that alarming night.

It had been a difficult few days. She felt herself pulling away and becoming more distant from Ross. Small things had started to niggle. If she was honest, she had begun to find a good deal of what Ross said to be quite annoying. She caught herself scrutinising his speech and finding him repeating himself again and again, which only served to irritate her. It was understandable to feel this way, of course. He had asked a great deal of her, and she had been forced to compromise her principles because of it. Recurrently though, she lifted her spirits, thinking of Ross's inheritance and the dream awaiting them when this was over. For now, anyway, life had to go on. Kinnaven had suffered a blow just as she had, but people were adjusting to life and so must she.

Jean knew that the medical practice had shut its doors out of respect following the old doctor's death. She presumed that the next town had taken any emergency patients. Now though, it being three days since the body was found, the health centre had opened once more, and this, of course, meant her services were required. She was glad to return, finding comfort in talking about the dreadful incident with others who had known the woman. Still, it seemed inexplicable that a person of such standing in the community would choose such a way to die. Surely, Jean thought, doctors possessed other means to put an end to things. There were pills and injections of all sorts. You saw it on television all the time.

The receptionists voiced much the same opinion when she arrived. She slipped off her jacket and putting her tabard on, went through to the front before beginning her work, feeling that she could hardly go about her business without speaking first. It was before the surgery had opened to the public, many of whom, Jean guessed, would also be asking themselves the same questions as her. No doubt the girls working at the front desk would be asked again and again if they had had any idea that the doctor was going to do such a thing.

'I can't even think about it,' Frances said. 'Goodness knows how we carry on today. The other doctors were in a long meeting yesterday, probably discussing how to reorganise things. God knows there are so many booked in already to see her, and what do we do with them all?'

Jean nodded. 'I can't believe she did it. I thought I knew her better than some, having cleaned her house, but I had no idea.'

'No one did,' said Anita, the other receptionist. 'Even the rest of the GPs, and surely out of all of us, they should know. They're trained to spot the signs, aren't they? I took in their refreshments yesterday during a meeting and caught the end of what Dr Davage was saying. Close to tears, she was, saying she should have spotted it. How anyone could have known though, I don't understand. When someone decides, that's it. No one can blame themselves for it.'

'I suppose not,' Jean said.

'The police have been in asking questions,' Frances went on. 'I had wondered if they thought there was something fishy about it all. Dr Davage was talking to them for over an hour the other day. I heard they were in Dr Cosgrove's house too, the day following her death. Jean, did you know about that?'

Jean's face reddened. 'Why would I?' she asked. 'I don't know any more than you about it all.'

'I thought as you cleaned the house, they might have spoken to you,' Frances said. 'I assume they were satisfied with what Dr Davage told them though. There's been no mention of any further inquiries, have there?'

Jean knew that she had already made a foolish slip and hoped that the other girl would put it down to nerves.

'Anyway,' Frances said, 'I think there's a remembrance service planned at the church. I don't go up there, as a rule. You know what that minister's like when he gets going, but I'll attend, of course. I've no idea about the funeral though. Do the police do a post-mortem when it's suicide? I suppose they must. And would she be buried or cremated? I don't know.'

'She had no relatives, did she?' Jean asked.

'No one close, as far as I know,' Frances said. 'She rarely had visitors either. Very private woman. Her work was her life. So sad.'

Suddenly, Jean had a thought. 'She owned the practice, didn't she? I mean the building. I wonder who it'll go to.'

Frances looked supremely self-satisfied. She leaned forward. Both Anita and Jean found themselves matching her movement and when Frances spoke it was in an exaggerated whisper. 'Last week,' Frances said. 'Raised voices.' The receptionist pointed to Dr Ruth Davage's door.

'When was this?' asked Anita.

'You were off and Zoe was on her break,' Frances answered, clearly annoyed to be interrupted so soon into her story. 'It was only me and that boyfriend of yours, Jean. We were both behind the desk working. Anyway, there were raised voices and I admit, I did need to fetch a leaflet from the waiting room and I might have hovered by the door.'

Anita and Jean exchanged knowing looks, and Frances grinned. 'Well, it's a damn boring place to work, for the most part,' she said. 'Little wonder I did have a listen.'

'Go on then, what were they saying?' asked Anita.

'The retirement was the topic, as it has been these last few months. Stubborn about it, the old doctor and not willing to hand over the reins to Dr Davage, that's how it seemed to us, wasn't it, Anita? Anyway, I wonder if Dr Davage had finally challenged her on it. Perhaps, she gave her a few home truths. We all knew she was nearing the end of her career. There have been several complaints. I shouldn't really say,' the receptionist said with false diplomacy, but this was wasted on Jean for she had no interest in the doctor's fitness to practice. 'Anyway,' Frances went on, 'I didn't catch it all, but there was talk about the building, just as you mentioned, Jean. I heard Dr Davage say that she was remortgaging her house to buy it over, or something of the sort. I assumed that was what the old doctor had asked her to do. It made sense, but then I heard Dr Cosgrove's reply.' Frances allowed for a dramatic pause. When finally she went on, she had lowered her voice further. 'Almost shouted, the old doctor did. I can still hear her voice now,' she said with enjoyment. '"Not over my dead body," Dr Cosgrove said. "It's still an interest of mine even if I don't practice here and it'll stay that way. God knows what you were thinking, Ruth."'

Jean was the first to speak. 'What did she mean, then?'

'I thought about it afterwards,' Frances said. 'I guess she'd wanted to keep ownership of the building and rent it out to the doctors who continued practising here. Still, even though she'd planned to retire, she couldn't let it go.'

'I see.' Jean nodded. 'And that might get tiresome for the others, having to go to her for permission to do this, that or the next thing, I suppose.'

'Yes,' said Frances. 'It certainly didn't go down well with Dr Davage, anyway. Went flouncing out, you know how she does when she's got a bee in her bonnet. Slammed her consulting room door and didn't come out until I called through to tell her that her afternoon patients were complaining about the wait.'

'So, Dr Cosgrove was fairly wound up,' Jean summarised.

'I thought your lad would have told you that anyway,' Frances said.

'Oh, if there was an argument in the room, I doubt he'd have noticed,' Jean said. 'Not if he was working at the shelves behind the desk. When he's on a job, he's quite focused.'

Frances snorted. 'I didn't mean that,' she said. 'I meant about Dr Cosgrove calling him into her room at the end of the day. Goodness knows what it was about, but he left in a hurry and didn't even tidy up what he was doing either. Tell him when you see him, that I had to clear away his shelving packs and the tools and screws. Nearly went over my ankle, tripping on it.'

'I'll tell him,' Jean said, hoping her answer sounded easy. 'Now, I'd better get on. This place won't clean itself.'

As she polished the waiting room, frantic thoughts raced through her mind. Why hadn't Ross told her that he had spoken to the old doctor the afternoon before she had died? What possible reason could he have? And what had they spoken about anyway? Had the doctor simply wanted to ask Ross how the job was going, or had she even planned to extend his employment? Surely then, he would have told her immediately. But, of course, he hadn't been home that night, he had stayed at the farmhouse. For the first time, Jean felt absolute panic. Her mouth went dry, and she dropped the cloth she was holding and stood stock-still. Supposing the doctor had realised that the missing £150 had not been a simple administrative error made by Frances. Imagine she had somehow known it was Ross, after all. What if Ross had been sacked or at least threatened with dismissal? And then, a far worse thought came to her. As she stood in the Kinnaven doctors' surgery, she wondered for the first time if Ross might have been involved in the doctor's death. Try as she might, she could not eliminate the thought from her mind. It returned throughout the morning, looming larger and larger.

Things didn't add up. She wished Ross was there so that she could ask him why he hadn't spoken about the conversation at the practice. The more she thought about it, the more suspicious it seemed. It must have been a fairly major fall out for Ross to simply abandon his tools, the ones she had essentially paid for with her savings. They were Ross's only source of income currently, so it seemed inexplicable for him to leave them at the practice even if he had been sacked.

Jean went about the rest of her daily rounds with a terrible sense of foreboding. Following the doctors, she headed up to the minister's house to dust the multitude of wooden ornaments and his dreadful bookcase full of dull volumes. The minister was out, thank God, and she was free to wander through her duties in a distracted manner without cross-examination.

She received a text message from Ross while she was there. '£650!' it said. 'Thinking caps on for the next one.' Jean felt sick. How could Ross ask her to do it again? The message sowed a further seed of doubt in her mind. Could the doctor's threat of exposure have driven Ross to do something utterly abhorrent? Had she misread the situation the entire time? Had Ross returned from the army a killer? Might his time in combat have altered his already weak mind, skewing his sense of integrity completely? Had he seen the old doctor as an object to bulldoze? A fly in his ointment to squash and flick away with distaste?

Jean rubbed her forehead. No, she was wrong, of course. Ross was manipulative but surely not a murderer. The idea was absurd. She was just getting herself into a state about things. Admittedly, he had some explaining to do when he returned from Aberdeen, but how she had considered him as being involved in the doctor's death was impossible to imagine. There was, she reminded herself, the note that the doctor had left in her drawer, and that was all the proof that she needed. The doctor had sat down and written the thing herself, scrawling the clumsily thought-out obituary for herself, perhaps pondering as she did, whether she would have the guts to go through with the jump. Possibly, that was why she had written the date and time. It had given her an ultimatum almost so that she might not back out. Jean reminded herself also that even without this piece of evidence, the police had concluded that the death was suicide. They had decided not to pursue the matter any further so that was good enough for her.

As she continued to dust, she considered the odd circumstances. Had the old doctor, on the afternoon before her death, simply been tying up loose ends? Had she known that Ross was responsible for the theft from the kitty and decided that the matter must be resolved before she was no longer able? Yes, this might well be the case, but the argument with Dr Davage concerned her. Why hadn't Dr Cosgrove been generous with her practice partner? Surely, knowing that she was going to kill herself, she would have wanted to leave things on a good note. Jean hoped the building would be left to the other doctors and they would benefit in this way from the old doctor's death. She could only imagine that the reason Dr Cosgrove had been so grumpy that afternoon, was due to nerves. Maybe even then, she had been weighing up whether she should go through with her plan. Yes, that seemed to make more sense.

By the time Ross returned from Aberdeen, jubilant having pawned the doctor's assets, Jean felt distinctly embarrassed. How could she think of him in this way? Ross was quite right in what he had said to her the week before. She had changed, and probably not for the better. She suspected everyone and everything these days. What had been wrong with her, turning against Ross, her childhood sweetheart, the man she planned to marry?

He arrived home after six. She wondered why he had needed to stay on in Aberdeen having already made the trade, but again, she chastised herself for being mean and hoped he had enjoyed some time alone. It was, after all, a big ask expecting him to take on another man's son, and without question, that was what Ross had done. When Calum saw his new friend coming up the drive, he could hardly contain his excitement and ran to the door, ambushing him with a flurry of playful punches and battle-cries. Ross took it, as he always did, in very good spirit. Jean could see that he looked drained, but still, he swept the boy up and carried him through to the living room, telling him that Commander Ross would take no insolence from subordinates and he must pay the forfeit. Ten push-ups and then he must fetch him a beer from the fridge.

When Calum was finally in bed and they were able to talk, Jean began hesitantly. She broached the subject of the conversation she now knew he had had with Dr Cosgrove on the afternoon of her death. Nothing could have prepared her for his reaction though. Getting up stiffly and smoothing the creases from his jeans, he walked to the door.

'Ross?' she asked. But stony-faced and without saying a word, he left the house.

22

'I won't listen to any excuses,' he said. 'Get dressed. I'm taking you out. No arguments.'

Cathy smiled and stepped back to allow him into the cottage. 'I'm not the best company. It's been a rough few days. Well, weeks, actually.'

Ross pointed to the bathroom. 'In, shower and freshen up. You look a mess. I'll be waiting in the kitchen. Jeans are fine for where we're going.'

She hadn't the will to fight. As she quickly showered and dressed, she smiled to herself. Perhaps Ross was right. She had spent enough time moping alone. She was bored of her own company, going over and over her past mistakes and that dreadful vision of the doctor's body at the base of the cliffs. Maybe distraction was the best course of action after all.

Cathy had received a visit from one of the police officers dealing with Dr Cosgrove's death. He explained that the procurator fiscal was content to give a verdict of suicide without her appearing in person at the inquiry. It was an unpredictable event and no lessons were to be learned. Dr Cosgrove's partners at the practice had been cleared of any blame, even if they might personally feel it, in having missed the potential signs of suicidal ideation. The doctor had left no note and the post-mortem revealed no incurable illness suggesting a motive for the jump. Still, the procurator fiscal had concluded that the old lady, being so private, had made her choice without consulting anyone. Although it didn't sit well with Cathy, it seemed that there was little more to be said on the matter.

When she came through, Ross had poured a glass of wine for her. She noticed he was having a soft drink, presumably, planning to drive.

'I helped myself,' he said.

'So I see.' She smiled and took the glass.

'You look better,' he said and kissed her on the cheek without her having a chance to know what he was doing.

'Thanks.' She stepped back and grimaced as she took her first sip. 'Bit oaky,' she said with a laugh.

'Drink up quickly, we're heading out.'

'Where are you taking me?' she asked, gulping the rest of the wine.

'It's a surprise. I've got Iain's car.'

He was, in every way, the perfect gentleman. He led her to the car, taking her arm, opening the door and closing it for her. Already, she felt slightly giddy from the drink. She fumbled with her seat belt, but even that, Ross attended to, fastening the clip and bending in once more to kiss her again, but this time, lightly on the lips. Things were moving at an alarming rate, but as they drove to the next town and parked by the jetty, Cathy felt powerless to do a thing.

The harbour was quiet. Along the front were what must have once been fishermen's cottages, all quaint and picturesque. A pub with the unoriginal name of The Ship Inn was at the far side. She had a flash of recognition from fifteen years ago. Hadn't she and Suzalinna sat outside with a drink? She thought of her friend, so far away now, and experienced a stab of regret that she had found herself feeling so detached. Suzalinna had repeatedly attempted to call her this past week and when Cathy had answered, she had begged for her to talk more freely, but she had been in an almost dreamlike state. It was rather like listening to someone through a haze of background noise. Suzalinna's usual cheerful chatter only served to mildly irritate her. She felt as if her friend's voice was too loud, or her speech too forceful. When they did talk, Cathy wanted nothing more than to hang up and be left in peace. Suzalinna had already expressed a wish to join her, perhaps the following week when she had holiday leave. But much to Suzalinna's dismay, Cathy had suggested she defer.

Cathy sighed and Ross looked at her. Together they walked without speaking, looking at the few boats moored in the harbour. She was glad he didn't force any conversation. He seemed to know that she didn't want to speak, and was himself, comfortable with their silence. She had sobered up now and the cold air made her shiver. He drew her closer to him, wrapping an arm around her shoulders.

'You'll think I'm a cheapskate suggesting a chippy but I promise it's more than that,' he said.

They stood outside the shop. The tang of vinegar and grease was heavy in the air.

'Yes?' Ross asked, and she nodded and smiled. There seemed nothing more natural. Having paid for their suppers, he handed her a newsprint packet. The heat of the contents warmed her hands. Already she felt the paper clammy from the steam.

'Just up here,' he said. 'You'll be glad you made the walk.'

They continued in amicable silence. The road took them up a steep back street that climbed above the houses. When they were finally seated on the stone steps that wound intimately up past the old part of town, they looked out onto a perfect view of the surrounding countryside and shoreline.

'Worth it?' he asked.

She nodded.

The informal supper, eaten on their knees as they huddled together, seemed to liberate her and she found herself asking Ross how things had been up at the farmhouse since they last spoke. He finished chewing and wiped his fingers on the newsprint.

'It's settled down, I suppose,' he said. 'My father's been under the weather recently, and I guess that's pushed Alison's little hysterical outburst into the background. Obviously, there's been all the stuff with that woman jumping too.'

Cathy nodded. 'Horrible,' she said. 'Did your family have much to do with her?'

Ross shook his head. 'Alison had been in to see her since the baby was born and she looked after my father, of course. Not that she could do much to help with the arthritis. You'd know about that though.' He nudged her elbow and smiled. 'Not missing work then, or is it fine to be away?'

It was the first time he had asked her about it and she felt shy answering. 'I miss it a lot,' she said and swallowed. He didn't ask any more. She gazed out to sea. 'You must love it here,' she said after a while. 'Do you walk along the cliffs and make the most of it when you're home, or have you seen it so often that you forget to look?'

'What a funny way of putting it,' he said. 'I suppose you're right. No, I don't, as it happens. Since coming home, I've only walked the road to your cottage and not been to the cliffs themselves at all. Perhaps I should.'

Cathy smiled absently. How strange that he had lied. She knew he had been there. She had seen. Ross had more secrets than perhaps he let on, but she allowed it to pass. It was none of her business, anyway.

The evening was drawing in and shivering, Cathy pulled her jacket close about her.

'Home again, I think,' Ross said. 'You're getting cold. We can continue our chat back at the cottage.'

He drove home swiftly. As they approached the farm, Cathy touched his arm. 'Can you stop here? I'm still to pay Alison for this week and I need to check she's okay with me staying on.'

Ross pulled in. 'I'll leave you to it,' he said. 'Tap on the back door, they'll be in the kitchen, most likely. I need to see my father and then I'll drive you down to the cottage.'

Cathy had knocked and was waiting for someone to come when she heard a shout and then footsteps running. Ross came half-falling around the side of the house.

'Cathy! My father... I think he's dead.'

Together, they ran to the cottage. His words came breathlessly and slightly disjointed, but calmly, she asked him to slow down. Her questions were curt and closed. 'How did you find him? Does he have a history of illness other than arthritis? Has he recently been to the doctor for anything?'

Iain was standing in the courtyard, looking confused. Ross called out. 'Iain, did you hear what I said? Call nine nine nine. Dad's unwell.'

Iain started to ask what he meant, but stopped and ran towards the farmhouse, stumbling on the gravel as he did so.

Cathy shouted after him. 'Iain? Sorry. After that, can you run down and get a blue bag from my car?' She tossed him her keys. Iain disappeared into the house. Alison then joined them at the door, clearly having heard the commotion, and seeing her father-in-law lying prostrate on the floor, she began to falter.

'Alison,' Cathy said, 'was he unwell this evening?'

The other woman looked about wildly, her eyes darting

across the room. Cathy wondered if she was going to faint. 'Oh God! We didn't notice anything. His arthritis was bad all day. He saw the doctor recently. He had painkillers. I don't know. Was he on something for his blood pressure too? I don't know. Is he dead?'

Cathy and Ross had already half-dragged the man from his awkward position on the rug. His skin was mottled and purple. *Warm still*, Cathy thought, and, now that he was flat, and before even checking his airway and pulse, she raised her hand high and, making a fist, hammered him hard in the centre of his chest.

'Precordial thump,' she said as much to herself as Ross. 'He's no pulse or breathing. Has Iain called the ambulance yet?' Alison said he had. 'Good. Good,' Cathy said.

The old farmer's head was tilted back, his chin now lifted. Cathy noticed that his neck was less mobile than she would have liked. Probably because of his arthritis. She would still have room to secure an airway if Iain hurried with the bag. She moved around, positioning herself at his head, and looking down the length of his body while Ross crouched by her.

'You're okay doing chest compressions, right?' she asked. 'Thirty to two, okay? I've got his airway.'

Ross was not confident but he did as she asked, kneeling by his father's side, and placing his interlinked fingers on the chest. He rested the heel of his hand centrally.

'Higher,' Cathy said and moved his hands an inch or so further up, only then allowing him to begin. She told him at once to slow down. 'You'll be knackered if you keep going at that rate,' she explained. He nodded without speaking.

Iain ran in with the knapsack and smiling up, Cathy thanked him and told him to step back. Already kneeling by the man's side, she had snapped on a pair of gloves. She dipped two fingers into his mouth, checking for any debris. 'Bag and mask,' she said to herself, but Iain had already found them and was handing them to her. Thank God she had brought the cumbersome knapsack in her car. It took up half her boot space and she had almost left it at home.

'Push the knapsack closer, will you?' she said, and Iain stepped forward and manoeuvred it to within her reach. She glanced up at him and Alison. They both looked dreadful. Iain had covered his face with his hands. 'Go outside,' she told them. 'You don't need to watch this. Go and look out for the ambulance coming, and wave them in.'

They left, and while Ross was compressing his father's chest, Cathy rummaged in the bag for a laryngeal mask, to make for a more reliable airway, especially if the man was to be transported by ambulance.

'Shit, Cathy,' Ross said. He was panting now, but still keeping count.

'Do you need a rest?' she asked. 'We'll swap over in a minute once I get his airway sorted. Then all you'll need to do is squeeze the bag.'

After giving him two more breaths with the bag, she lifted it and the mask free of his face, and while Ross again set to with his chest compressions, she slotted in the laryngeal mask, in one smooth movement. 'Okay. We're good,' she said. 'Let me take over.'

But he wouldn't. He was in a rhythm now, and there was nothing she could do, other than to encourage him. 'They'll be here soon,' she said. 'I'd like to get a line in if I could before they get here. We'll do it between breaths. Ross, keep counting out loud for me.'

By the time the ambulance arrived, she had gained venous access. The paramedics didn't hang about, shocking him with the defibrillator four times before they went. A 'scoop and run', was what Cathy and her colleagues would have called it. Iain followed in the Land Rover.

And then, everything seemed suddenly very still. The blue lights illuminated the fields and the hedgerows as they passed. Iain's cows, the cows that had been started by his grandfather, the line then carried on by his father, looked up languidly as the ambulance and its convoy sped past, their mouths moving in a slow circular motion as they chewed. Some of Kinnaven's residents came out of their houses to watch. Jean stood on her doorstep and wondered what might be going on.

Cathy and Ross saw the intermittent blue weave the narrow lanes and then pick up speed as it reached the main road in the distance.

'Shit,' he said softly.

She reached out a hand, but he turned from her. She couldn't blame him. They both knew that his father would not return to the farm.

23

Jean shook with anger. What had Ross thought he was playing at? He had barely spoken to her since his father had died.

And to think that originally, she had been idiotically pleased on hearing the news that the old farmer had passed. Of course, she wouldn't have wished ill on anyone, but the death seemed undeniably convenient for them. It spelt an end to Ross's financial difficulties, and it should have signalled the beginning for their own life together, just as he had promised. Jean had been hurt by Ross's reaction last week when he had refused to explain himself over his interview with Dr Cosgrove, but she had been quite prepared to put it down to stress. She still couldn't understand why he had snubbed her, but during the hours of speculating and worrying it over, she concluded it must have been due to embarrassment on his part. He had been sacked, of course, and couldn't admit it.

The few days before the funeral had dragged for her, and she had questioned if she should approach him and try to make amends, but knowing that it was he who was in the wrong, she had stubbornly waited, growing more and more anxious. Calum had asked for him, wanting to show his new friend a trick he had learned with his football, but she had told him that Ross needed time alone to grieve.

She had assumed it would change after the funeral. That would be when he would come and talk to her, and they would pick up where they had left off. But this had not happened, and Ross had essentially ignored her and her mother. Even her mum had noticed and commented. When Jean had arrived at the church, she had watched as Ross and the rest of the family chatted at the front. After all that had happened between them, Jean felt that she should have been included, perhaps not in the family party, but she should've at least been given some sort of extra nod. Had Ross come forward and greeted her and her mum, ushering them to a nearby seat, that would have been enough. But, of course, he had not and had barely made eye contact with her either. Bloody cheek.

This was bad enough, but following the service, when they had moved on to the pub, he had then point-blank refused to come to her side of the bar. She had tried to put on a brave face, chatting with her mother and Cathy, who had come to stand beside them. She thought she had been quite restrained but then, that silly Frances girl from the doctors had come over at the end of the night. She had been half-cut and stupid, and had rudely asked Jean if things had cooled between her and Ross because a friend of hers had seen him in the next town only the week before eating chips with some other girl! Jean, who at that point was standing alone, her mother and Cathy having left long ago, stalked from the pub, tramping all the way home with ever-increasing rage.

As the evening drew in and she waited for Ross's knock at the door, Jean brooded. She had had too much to drink that day. Her mother and Cathy had known when to stop, but she had kept on going. That Cathy was a funny one. Nice, but a bit fragile. Shrewd, Jean thought. Definitely that. Shrewd and clever. She wondered if Ross had noticed her and the young doctor chatting. He'd have been surprised, no doubt, to see her getting on with someone so smart.

Jean crossed the bedroom unsteadily and looked out at the darkened sky. A lump lodged in her throat. Wine always made her maudlin. She shouldn't have touched the stuff. Supposing, now that the time had come, Ross shirked his proposal. He hadn't made anything official, and neither of them had spoken publicly about the engagement. What was to stop him from taking up with whoever he might fancy now he had money to enjoy? Jean imagined him selling up his half of the farm to the housing developers who had already been bargaining with the old farmer for years. She knew that the old man must have been tempted, but he had been loyal to his land it seemed and had refused to budge. Ross would have no such scruples. She could imagine him selling up and living the playboy lifestyle. He'd never stay on in Kinnaven. All of their plans, the sacrifices she had made for him, and it was just a sham. Jean wished she could expose him for the man he was: the liar, the player, the master manipulator. How could she have been so gullible? She had ignored her morals for him, turned her back on who she was.

Her phone buzzed. It was him. Coward. Couldn't he face her? She threw it down on the bed, but it continued to ring. Snatching it up again, she answered.

'Yes?'

'That's hardly...'

'It's been a long day for all of us, Ross.'

He sighed. 'Darling... I've had too much to drink. I was going to come round. If you're in a huff about...'

'In a huff? In a bloody huff?' Her voice rose a semitone and knowing that she might wake Calum, she tried to gain control of herself once more. 'Why might I be in a huff, Ross? I wonder why you'd suggest it. Perhaps the fact that you ignored both my mother and me. And then I hear you've been cavorting with someone else. My God! When I think of all I've done for you since you came back to this bloody village. When I think of the sacrifices I've made. I welcomed you into my home. I got you a bloody job. I abandoned my better judgement all for you. If you think I'll allow you to treat me this way...'

He was laughing. A low, quiet, sardonic laugh.

'What?' she said, incandescent with rage. 'What the hell are you laughing for?'

'Oh Jeanie, Jeanie,' he said in a sing-song voice. 'I do love it when you get like this.'

'You'll not love it when I go to the police!'

Silence. She waited, her breathing shallow and her mind racing.

His tone had changed when he spoke. Before, his words had been slightly slurred, but now he was quite clear.

'You know, that wouldn't be so smart, Jean,' he said. 'For one, it was you who pocketed old Mrs Spratt's money, wasn't it? It was you who sneaked into the dead doctor's house too. Darling, I don't want to labour the point, but you'll not be going to the police anytime soon, will you?'

She didn't speak. How could she answer?

'Darling, let's not fall out. That wasn't what I wanted at all. I'm busy for the next few days but when I'm done...'

She ended the call, throwing her phone down on her pillow.

Oh, how clever he had been. The thefts, all bar the one at the doctors' surgery, for which it seemed Ross had already met his comeuppance, had been completed by her. Jean moaned. She was completely at his mercy and would be for the rest of her life. He could blackmail her endlessly, saying that he was going to her mother, or even the police, with the sordid tale. Although she had benefited little from the thefts, it was she who had undertaken them. What had she been thinking? Oh, what a fool she had been! How could she have been so stupid, so trusting? And to think that she was planning her life with him, placing her future happiness in his hands, calling him her soulmate. Oh God, what an idiot. But with this in mind, a new feeling came. If she had been jealous and angry before, she was seething with fury now. He had trapped her completely.

When she awoke the next morning, admittedly with a crushing hangover, but also with a seed of an idea. Something had been bothering her about both the doctor's death and that of Ross's father. Ross had been edgy, as if he had something to hide. Jean knew both deaths had in some way benefited him. The doctor might have exposed his theft and caused his father to write him out of the will, and his father, of course, had left him half the farm. Jean knew she had been a fool to steal, but she felt sure that if Ross had been involved in the deaths, his crime was far worse. Getting up and moving to the bathroom, she felt sure that something was wrong with the two deaths. She knew she didn't have the brains to untangle Ross's wrong-doing, he was too clever by far, but she had a friend. She hurriedly showered and then smiled at her reflection in the mirror. How glad she was that Cathy had arrived in town. She was not so close to the situation that she would be biased and was undoubtedly highly intelligent. Drying herself, Jean concluded that Cathy was just the person to consult on the matter of a suspected double murder. Far safer to go to her than the police, that was for sure. She would know what to do.

She was heading to the farm let later that day and made up her mind to broach the subject one way or another. But as she did her rounds, visiting one of her old ladies and then the minister's house, she began to worry. What if they did discover that Ross had been involved in some way with the death of the doctor and his father? Of course, initially, it might keep her own secret safe, but if he was arrested and convicted, what was to stop him blowing the whole thing and telling the police about her lawbreaking too? Jean thought about this a good deal until a further point occurred to her. Might there be a way to allow Cathy to investigate the possible crimes, without Ross's knowledge of her involvement? Suppose she was in a position to insinuate his guilt, yet stay superficially devoted to him, could she then come away unscathed? It was a fragile but definite possibility, and she cleaned the minister's crumbling old books with renewed fervour.

But was he guilty? If the police had written off both deaths as being without suspicion, how on earth could she prove otherwise? Then again, the police hadn't even considered murder in either case, and why should they? Superficially, no one would benefit from the doctor's passing. The doctor's death had been clear cut and other than the lack of explanation as to why she should end her life at that time, there was no reason to suspect foul play. Then there was Ross's father, a man known to be in frail health and known also to be fond of a drink. What could be more plausible than him dying suddenly of a heart attack? Both deaths benefited one person alone – and that was Ross. If he had killed either one, Jean had no idea how he had done it. She cast her mind back to the night of the doctor's death. Ross had not stayed with her that night, she remembered that well. Might then Iain, or even Alison, be able to shed some light on his movements? Jean didn't know how to go about finding this out without drawing attention to herself. Again, she thought of Cathy. Being far more intellectual and able than her, she was surely the best person to ask.

As Jean continued her journey down through the village and out towards Kinnaven Farm and the sea, she wondered how to introduce the topic. It was important to keep Cathy as neutral as possible and she most definitely didn't want her to think that she was some jealous girlfriend out to seek revenge on her man having been wronged, however true that might be. And then another idea occurred to her. Reaching into her jacket pocket, she drew out the folded paper. Why she had taken it with her that morning she could not say. It had been in the bathroom cabinet these past few days, hidden there in case Ross had gone through her coat looking for money, but he hadn't been home and she had retrieved it thinking that she might show it to her mum after the funeral. She had had second thoughts about that, realising that in showing it, she would, of course, implicate herself in having been in the doctor's house following her death, and for the sake of giving a thrill to her mother, it wasn't worth the risk. Today though, if she worded it carefully, she could introduce her doubts to Cathy. She would say that she had accidentally come upon the letter while clearing the doctor's house the day before her death. Without question, the note was strange. She would show it to Cathy. She might word it cleverly. Perhaps she could say that it seemed odd that both the doctor and farmer had died in quick succession. That should supply Cathy with enough intrigue to start digging.

When Jean arrived at the cottage, her stomach flipped. She was not usually a nervous person but in taking this step and starting a potential investigation into the deaths, she knew that she was crossing a line. What if that evening, Ross turned up on her doorstep full of remorse? What if he was keen to take up where they had left off? Jean knew that she was weak and, in her heart, she still loved him, but she was a great believer in fate and this was how she framed the situation in her mind. If Ross was innocent of involvement in the deaths, and if he returned to her with an explanation for his behaviour, all well and good. If, however, he was guilty of cheating on her, or worse than that, murder, then how could she consider having a relationship with him? She thought of little Calum and how disappointed he would be to hear that Ross wasn't returning to play, but far better that than endangering her young son.

When Cathy answered the door, Jean's mind was made up, she smiled a little tensely and went in with her cleaning products in one hand and the doctor's letter in the other.

~

Cathy looked up having read the note, and at that moment Jean wondered if she had made a mistake.

'Where did you say you got this?' she asked seriously, her lips as pale as her face.

Jean tried to be as offhand as she could. 'I know what you're saying, Cathy,' she said. 'It's all done with and the police are happy and all that, but something just irked, if you know what I mean? I found the note the day before. It went out of my head, and to be fair, it doesn't really say anything to suggest a reason for her killing herself; it's as if she's been practising an obituary for herself, don't you think? Or maybe you think there's something odd about it too? You see, I have a feeling there's something wrong, but I can't work out what. I know we're too late to hand it in to the police, and the doctor's dead and buried, but then when the old farmer died so soon afterwards, I panicked and thought the deaths might be somehow linked. That sounds stupid, doesn't it?'

Cathy's face twitched and Jean watched as yet an unknown emotion passed across her countenance. Finally, a smile crept at the corners of the young woman's mouth.

'You've got a bee in your bonnet, that's for sure,' Cathy said, and only then, Jean breathed a sigh of relief. She knew she had done the right thing coming here. Cathy would get to the bottom of it all for her and she might sit back and watch things unfold.

24

W hen Jean left, Cathy spent some time gazing out the window at the sea. Her curiosity had certainly been aroused. She turned the idea over and over in her mind. Had either of the deaths been suspicious? That was what Jean had suggested. The reason for the cleaner thinking it was still unclear but, if truth be told, she had already begun to wonder the same. Over the past few weeks, she had observed too many idiosyncrasies. Things in Kinnaven, the people, the place as a whole, just didn't seem quite right. She had assumed that this impression came from her being hypersensitive or emotional. She had wondered if the peculiarity was coming solely from the farm and had, perhaps unfairly, considered that Alison might be going through some kind of a postnatal depressive episode and that this attitude might have filtered to those around her in some way. But now that Jean had also voiced a concern, she felt sure that there was something more.

Cathy crossed to the kitchen counter and looked down at the note. Jean had admitted taking the letter from the old doctor's house the day before her death. Why had she done such a thing? Had she intended on returning the paper, or did she have some other plan? Cathy considered Jean's character. She had only known her a short time, but had instinctively liked the woman for her open and bright attitude and her reliable nature. Was it conceivable that Jean had taken the note hoping to gain something? Might she have planned to show it to old Dr Cosgrove and blackmail her? Cathy thought this unlikely, but to take something from someone's house made her wonder. Had Jean taken anything else? Certainly, *she* had missed nothing following Jean's visits, but had anyone else in the village? It was an ugly thought and one which Cathy fought with, but it was a possibility.

Cathy considered this, recalling Jean's jovial banter in the pub on the previous day, and saw it in perhaps a different light. Twice, Jean had called her a cheapskate. Of course, it was a joke, and she had laughed and bought the next round of drinks, but had there been more to it than that? A cleaner's wage must be relatively low, although Jean herself always looked to be well enough off. Cathy had seen that she owned a model of mobile phone far newer than her own so things couldn't be that desperate, but then again, had this been funded by illegal means? Cathy snorted aloud. How melodramatic. But what a temptation, to have access to so many people's houses and to be there alone with their belongings. How easy it might be to pocket something small, knowing that it would be likely to go unnoticed.

But if Jean was a thief, it didn't dispel the fact that there had been two recent deaths in Kinnaven. Both had been unexpected and the suicide of Dr Cosgrove, in particular, did not sit easily with her. She had met Dr Cosgrove and already felt a strong connection to the woman. Although, at the time, she had despised the way her consultation had played out, she knew that the other doctor had been right. Dr Cosgrove had saved her from herself that day. Had she simply written out a prescription for dihydrocodeine to save the awkwardness of saying no, Cathy might well have taken the lot and be at the bottom of the cliffs now herself. No, she decided, if there was something odd about Dr Cosgrove's death, she couldn't leave it.

She thought of Jean and the problem she had left her with. For the time being, she consciously decided to ignore the young cleaner's potentially petty involvement. Jean's motive for consulting her remained unclear, though. Cathy assumed that Jean herself suspected that either one or both of the deaths had been murder. She wondered if the cleaner had an idea of who the perpetrator might be but felt powerless to say. Could it be that she feared someone close to her might be wrongly accused and, in asking for her help, she hoped to clear their name? Cathy felt this was unlikely. Both deaths had already been accepted as unsuspicious. If Jean simply said nothing, then the matter would be resolved. Perhaps then, the opposite was true. Did Jean hope to implicate someone in the crime for some reason, and wish that Cathy might do the job for her? Did she suspect someone and believe Cathy would come to the same conclusion and bring the offender to justice? She assumed that Jean had come to her in particular with some real purpose. The cleaner's interest in convincing her, or the rest of Kinnaven, that the deaths had been suspicious, seemed to be vital. Although not wholly satisfied with this theory, Cathy accepted that she was unlikely to get any further with it.

She made herself a small meal and attempted to clear her mind of all judgements or thoughts of the business. This she knew was the only way in which she might come at the matter fresh and unflustered that afternoon. Having cleared away the dishes, she sat down in the living room in a comfortable chair, with a pen and paper to hand, intending to jot down any ideas that occurred to her. First, she thought, she must take both deaths as separate entities, as currently, she had no evidence to link the two. Perhaps during her consideration, this might become clearer.

Dr Cosgrove was first and had, it seemed, left her house with the sole intention of walking to her death that dreadful night. The police had found no motive. She had no malignancy or life-limiting disease on post-mortem. Everything seemed to suggest that the doctor might look forward to a well-earned retirement in the village she had served and loved. Cathy wondered if she had really been so delighted at the end of her career. She herself, although admittedly much younger, had considered the end of her profession as a grave and unwanted event. Cathy thought back to her own near-jump that morning and shivered. This was as legitimate a reason for the doctor killing herself as she had come upon so far.

Cathy leaned back in her chair and sighed. She wasn't making much headway with it and all she had achieved was to convince herself that the old doctor had intentionally jumped because she couldn't imagine life after her vocation had ended. No, she decided. This was not a good enough reason to jump. She had bipolar, she was at a crossroads in her life and had been feeling confused and alone. She had been forced suddenly to reconsider everything about herself. That was her reason. The same could not be said for Dr Cosgrove.

Cathy looked at it again from a different angle. Had the doctor shown any signs of deterioration in mental health beforehand? She thought it might at least prove possible to ask around the village or perhaps interview someone working in the health centre. Jean seemed too close to the problem currently. Might someone else give her a better idea of how the old doctor had been behaving before her death? Cathy felt somewhat dispirited though, knowing that surely the police must have covered all of this ground already.

Assuming then, that the police had looked into things

thoroughly and the doctor had, according to those around her, been mentally well leading up to her apparent suicide, what then might the note that Jean had found mean? Jean had thought it was the doctor working on an obituary for herself. An odd thing for anyone to do, but perhaps conceivable if the writer intended to kill themselves soon and was seeking some resolution in the writing. Something about the note had been wrong though, both Jean and she had seen it.

Cathy got up from her armchair and went through to the kitchen where she had left it. Jean had folded it into four, but the paper seemed to have been creased twice more to make it, at some point, far smaller. She smoothed it out in front of her on the kitchen worktop.

'Dr Cosgrove will always be remembered for her courage during hard times. This time, however, the pain was too intense and she died by suicide at the local beauty spot, Devil's Leap on Wednesday 5th August at 11pm.'

Cathy couldn't say exactly why the note puzzled her. She paced around the kitchen, wracking her brains, but still, she couldn't come up with anything. In saying that the doctor had suffered hard times in the past, the note perhaps indicated she had experienced mental health issues before. Why then had the police not discovered this past issue? Surely it would have been common knowledge in such a small village if the doctor had required time off work for depression. Not once had Cathy ever heard mention of this on her travels.

She was getting annoyed with her stupidity. 'Think,' she repeated under her breath. 'Think.' She walked through to the living room once more. Suppose she took it as certain that the doctor had been murdered. Perhaps by working back the way, she might make sense of the note.

The doctor had walked to the cliffs, presumably without coercion. If she had been killed, someone must have crept up and pushed her over the edge. Cathy supposed that the police had found no footprints indicating that someone else had been on the moors. Certainly, when she had been out herself that morning, she had seen nothing. Then it occurred to her that the proposition of someone sneaking up on the doctor in the late evening was flawed. Number one, why push the doctor if she was standing on the clifftops all ready to jump herself? And two, unless she had been followed from her own house, how would any Kinnaven resident know that the doctor was headed to the cliffs in the first place? The more Cathy thought about this, the more ridiculous the entire thing seemed.

She spent much of the afternoon in this resolute state, refusing to move on to the farmer's death, and doggedly running over and over the events of the night the doctor jumped or had been pushed. When finally, the sun began to drop in the sky and shadows formed about the cottage, Cathy glanced up at the clock. She had been going at this for nearly four hours and so far, she had achieved nothing. Maybe she should admit defeat now and give the whole thing up. She might hand the note back to Jean and tell her that she wanted nothing to do with the business. She had thought it over and both deaths seemed quite plausible and innocent.

Cathy's bones ached. She looked around the dark room and her stomach rumbled. The pub served hot meals. Maybe the food would renew her energy. She could take a slow walk up through the village and have a quiet drink without bothering to cook anything herself. What time was it now? Five thirty. Cathy stared at the clock. And then it struck her. How could she have been so stupid? That was it, of course: the reason the note had seemed so strange. She fumbled on the table and finding the paper, reread it.

'...she died by suicide at the local beauty spot, Devil's Leap on Wednesday 5th August at 11pm.'

Why would anyone record the time of death in an obituary? It was wrong, completely wrong. Unless, of course, it wasn't the doctor that had written the letter but someone else entirely. If this was the case, the note might be read with a completely different meaning. Supposing the doctor had received this note, perhaps it had been pushed through her door anonymously. The implication, if this was the case, was grave indeed. Had the note specified a threat? Had the doctor been sent an invitation to her own death? A death by appointment?

25

Having handed over the problem to Cathy, Jean had hoped to feel some relief, but instead, she found herself jittery. What if she had made a mistake in confiding her suspicions? Cathy had initially seemed the ideal candidate to expose Ross, being an outsider and clever, but the more she thought about it, the more worried she became. It was all well to suspect Ross herself, but passing on those doubts to someone else seemed a big step. What if she was wrong and her own misdemeanours were exposed? If Cathy was that astute, she might easily discover everything.

When she received a message that evening from Cathy, asking to see her again as soon as possible, she felt both elated and sick. Of course, it might simply mean that the young doctor had decided the problem was beyond her and that she didn't want to investigate at all. If that was so, Jean felt that she too would let it drop. She would pretend that this entire sorry episode with Ross hadn't happened. She would push the two deaths to the back of her mind and attempt to get on with her life.

She asked her parents to babysit Calum. They'd been called upon a good deal more often since Ross's departure from the scene. Jean's mother, who had herself become pregnant with Jean's older brother, Matty, at a young age, was more sympathetic than her father.

'Let the girl go out for once,' she told her husband. 'She works hard enough during the week to provide for Calum. The least we can do is help occasionally.'

Jean's father had returned to his newspaper without comment other than a shake of his head.

And so, Jean found herself back at the holiday cottage for the second time that day, anxious to hear what Cathy had to say.

Cathy opened the door and welcomed her in. 'I'm just back from the pub actually,' she said and then laughed at Jean's look of surprise. 'I've become lazy cooking since I arrived here, not that I was much of a cook before, if I'm honest.'

It was not until they were both seated in the kitchen with their hot drinks that they spoke frankly.

'I've read the note you left and I know that you were puzzled about why the doctor might have written it. I saw something odd in it almost immediately too but it took me several hours to work out why.'

'And you know? Already? And the doctor's death and the old farmer?'

'That will take a bit more thought.' Cathy laughed. 'I don't know what you expect of me, Jean, but I'm not some Sherlock Holmes. I don't spirit philosophies from thin air.'

Jean smiled down at her tea.

'Before I look into things properly, and I think I would like to do so given that I had misgivings about Dr Cosgrove's death myself, I'd like to ask you one question. Please, you must be completely honest.'

Jean looked up abruptly. Was this when Cathy would ask about the thefts? Had she seen through her so easily? There was a silence, and she held Cathy's gaze, afraid to look away. When Cathy spoke, she did not say what Jean had expected.

'Why do you suspect Ross of murder?'

Jean inhaled sharply and stared about her wildly for a second or two.

'I see by your reaction that I'm right. I have to be honest with you, I needed to know from the start why you wanted me to investigate. You might just as easily have gone to the police and asked them, but I assumed it was too close to home. There had to be a reason for you stirring things up. I asked at the pub. It wasn't hard to find out. A few of the villagers and one of the barmaids filled me in. Ross and you have been seeing each other since he returned from the army, haven't you? I had no idea.'

Jean nodded. 'We've known each other since we were kids. We used to kick about together. Childhood sweethearts.' She smiled wryly. 'We lost touch when he joined up. I met someone else and had Calum, but when my marriage ended, I thought of him and wondered... Maybe I was being naive to think we could pick up where we left off as teenagers. Ross came home, not different from his old self, but changed all the same. It was as if he had lost something. He even said that himself. Maybe his integrity.' Jean inhaled slowly. 'To be fair, even back then, when we were kids, he was a bit wild. Used to get into trouble for minor things and then, as he got older, his mum and dad got pretty sick of bailing him out. The army was his escape. Kinnaven had become too small for him, and he needed to find his wings. I worried though, you know? His character. He was easily led.'

Cathy nodded. 'I think Ross's character is in question, undoubtedly. He has been far from truthful with you in many respects. That's between the pair of you, of course. But why then do you suspect him of being a killer?'

Jean shifted in her seat and sighed. She felt Cathy's eyes on her and knew she had to start somewhere. 'I don't believe it. I don't want to believe he is.'

'But why do you then? I can't look into this if I don't have the facts, can I? It'd be like starting with a disadvantage and that's not fair.'

'I've no proof whatsoever,' she said. 'All I know is that his character is questionable. He's not the person he likes to make out. He's manipulative. He can be controlling and scheming.'

Cathy nodded but didn't speak.

'I know the police are convinced that it's all fine, but I just wondered. Who benefits most from his father dying?'

'Well, if it's just the old farmer's death, then surely both he and his brother, not to mention his brother's wife, benefit financially. Didn't the old man split the farm equally between the two boys?'

Jean shook her head in frustration. 'I know all that, but he's been in serious trouble since he came home. Someone's been chasing him for money. He owes a debt. I think he's cleared it now, but he's still struggling. He even took some of my money without saying. Oh, I'm not talking about much, but we had an understanding, you know?'

'So, he had a reason for killing his father, although, as yet, we have no reason to believe he did so. What then? Why did he want to kill old Dr Cosgrove?'

Jean shrugged. In telling this, she might blow the whole thing. Admitting to having known that Ross was stealing from the surgery would place her in danger. How could she tell Cathy that his motive for killing the doctor was to keep the old woman quiet after she discovered the truth about the theft? If Dr

Cosgrove had then possibly threatened to inform his father, Ross would have undoubtedly been written out of the will. She thought of Calum, sitting at home with his grandparents. He would be so ashamed to have a mother with a criminal record. Jean doubted she would go to prison but she couldn't trust Ross to keep quiet about the other thefts. Even if she didn't go to jail, how would she continue to work in the village?

Cathy's voice cut into her thoughts. 'I hear from the local gossips that you were instrumental in Ross getting a job up at the doctors' surgery. You clean there yourself, I assume?'

Jean nodded. 'Yes. I've worked for the doctor for nearly five years now. I've never had a complaint, not once.'

'I wonder why you say that,' Cathy said. 'I have to be honest. I still feel like you're keeping something back. Won't you tell me what it is and save me the trouble of finding out? I thought we were friends. After I found the doctor lying there at the base of the cliffs, you couldn't have been more supportive. If you want my help, can't you be straight with me?'

Jean stared back defiantly. 'I've nothing to say. You're flustering me and putting words into my mouth. Why can't you ask Ross about it?'

They had reached a stalemate. She was glad to leave, but doing so, she felt uneasy. She had a horrible feeling that she had made a terrible mistake in saying so much.

When she arrived home, she tried to settle, but her thoughts were interrupted by a text message from Ross. She had hardly heard a thing from him since the funeral. She was disgusted at herself as her heart had leapt when she saw his name on the screen. *Pathetic*, she said to herself. And then, opening the message, she grew bitter. A real man would have had the decency to come to the house to talk. But if she was honest, she was glad she didn't have to face him. She didn't know how she would ever look at him again after what she had done. Scanning through the message, she felt any remaining guilt dissipate and her anger rise. The message was brief. He needed some space after losing his father. Jean deleted the message. No, she had been right to go to Cathy. He had strung her along with his lies for long enough. Ross deserved what was coming to him.

26

In a sense, Cathy was relieved. Maybe she was no further on having spoken with Jean, but she had revealed Jean's suspicion of Ross. True, she had already known this, having asked around the village and discovered about their relationship, but it felt important to have had it confirmed. Of course, it put her in a difficult position. She had been at the mercy of Ross's charms. It would not be long before Jean found out they had been the couple spotted together in the next town. Cathy felt a little queasy when she thought of how trusting she had been and how effortlessly Ross had played her. Thank God nothing more had happened between them.

But just because Ross was a flirt, it did not make him a murderer, no matter how much Jean seemed to wish it. Cathy thought of poor confused Jean and how hurt she must feel to attempt to prove him guilty. How would Jean feel now though knowing that Cathy too had been involved with the man she still loved? Cathy considered this, and how fine a line there was between love and hate. Jean, having felt aggrieved by Ross, had snapped so quickly into the more destructive emotion.

Cathy went over the problem once more. The only way in

which Ross might have been involved in the doctor's death was if he had written the note to her, provoking her to walk to the cliffs. Then he might have waited on the moor hoping that she would take the hint, and if she didn't do it herself, he might step forward and push her. The doctor must have had some reason to be persuaded though. A single note as an obituary, however nasty, could hardly result in such drastic action.

For the first time, Cathy wondered if there might have been other notes, a whole collection of menacing letters. It seemed unlikely but it might be possible to find out. Jean must have been in and out of the doctor's house cleaning and would surely have seen any handwritten envelopes. If the notes had been delivered to the doctor's work, it would be harder unless, of course, Jean could help her there also. She cleaned at the surgery so must know the receptionists. Cathy, from her own experience, knew that all letters would pass through their hands. The girls at her practice would go through the post every morning, opening any correspondence, other than the letters marked 'private' or 'personal' which would be left sealed in the doctors' mail trays to be read after surgery. Cathy decided that this was at least one line of inquiry to explore.

Still, though, she was at a loss as to why Ross might be involved. What could he have against the old doctor? He had worked briefly as a handyman at the surgery doing odd jobs and putting up shelving, but he would surely not have had much contact with Dr Cosgrove herself. Of course, he had only returned to the village recently and wouldn't have seen the doctor in years. If there had been an old feud between them, from when Ross was a young boy and 'wayward' as Jean described, surely that must have been forgotten by now. Cathy snorted. Of course, it made no sense at all. If the doctor had had any past grievance with the boy, or now man, she would hardly have offered him a job in the first place.

So, she had come up with no motive and only a possible means of killing the doctor, although, it was all conjecture. What then, if she considered the farmer's death? Surely, the opposite was true. Ross had the strongest possible motive, coming into an inheritance, and at a time when it seemed, according to Jean, that finances were tricky. The problem was that he had been in her own company that night, eating fish and chips in the next town. A foolproof alibi.

Cathy had already wondered why Ross had lied to her before. She knew that he had. She had physical evidence to prove it. Perhaps she should confront him with it tomorrow and attempt to move the investigation further. In the end, she went to bed exhausted but tossed and turned, worrying about how she could challenge Ross without muddying the waters.

When she did sleep, she dreamt that it was she who had died having jumped from Devil's Leap. She watched from above and saw her patients and friends going about their daily business after hearing the news. *A good bit of gossip for a couple of days*, she thought angrily as she looked down, and then they all seemed happy to accept what they were told. She woke early, with the sun touching the edge of her curtains, her mind filled with indignation for, not herself in the dream, but the reality of Dr Cosgrove.

That morning, determined to move things forward, she drove up to Jean's house for a quick word. Jean had pointed out the place after the farmer's funeral and although Cathy was sure she had it right, she was thankful when it was indeed the cleaner who answered the door and not some stranger. Jean looked surprised to see her but invited her in, and Cathy explained what she wanted, interrupted at times by Calum requiring chivvying for school.

'More notes to the house?' Jean asked. 'Not that I ever saw, and that one, I didn't see coming in the post either. It didn't have an envelope, you see? I gave it to you as it was. I was only in one day a week though, so I suppose they might have come.'

Cathy sighed. 'That's a pity. I had hoped it was a new lead. How about her work? Do you think you could find out?'

Jean looked horrified. 'What, but how would I? You mean rake about at the surgery, going through her things?'

Cathy laughed. 'Goodness no. I'd never ask you to do that. No, I meant you could ask the receptionists if there had been any personal mail in the weeks before her death. It's rare for GPs to get private letters sent to their place of work, so one of the office girls might have spotted one.'

She left Jean and Calum still squabbling over whether the boy should wear a raincoat to school, and decided her next stop should be Kinnaven Farm to arrange a meeting with Ross.

As she drove along Kinnaven's narrow streets once more, she thought of Jean's home life and the happy, chaotic scene of domesticity she had just left. She pulled onto the farm track but was forced to brake suddenly, having failed to see a man jogging ahead. It was a blind bend and the car, despite its low gear, was almost on top of him before she knew it. The wheels crunched as she jammed on the brake pedal, and she swore loudly as the bumper skidded close to the back of the figure. As he turned in anger towards her, she saw it was Ross. She put on the handbrake and got out.

'God, I'm so sorry. I nearly had you.'

Ross stood, hands-on-hips breathing hard, probably from the run rather than the near-death experience. Droplets of sweat clung to his fringe and face, and he shook his head, sending them flying. His T-shirt was damp around the shoulders and chest, and his legs spattered with mud.

'Thought you were in the business of saving lives, not ending them,' he said, removing an earphone, which emitted a tinny drumbeat. 'Need to get my fitness up again,' he went on, 'too many beers these last few weeks.'

'It's been an odd time. Do you want to come down for a chat later? I feel I've not had a chance to speak with you since your father.'

'Sure. Let me get showered and I'll come down. I think Iain and Alison want me out of the way just now anyway.'

Cathy wondered what he meant and if Alison was having another breakdown. She seemed incredibly unpredictable. As she released the handbrake, having given Ross a good head start, she considered for the first time if he might not have been truthful, or if, at the very least, he had exaggerated Alison's fluctuant mental state. But what possible reason could Ross have for making out that his sister-in-law was anything but happy and normal? Once again, Cathy had the feeling that she was being lied to about something.

By the time he came down to the cottage, a good two hours later, she had decided that she didn't care anymore. She was asking straight out. She needed to know the truth to clear the whole matter up. There was no reason not to now. She and Ross weren't ever going to be anything to one another. She had met men like him in the past. They were incredibly charming, but the act soon wore thin and their egotistical side rapidly shone through. She pitied poor Jean for having allowed herself to get so close.

'Tea?' she asked, almost daring him to refuse. It felt like all she did was drink tea at the moment but she needed to be doing something while she talked.

Ross didn't seem to notice and was leafing through a magazine sitting on the countertop. 'Sure,' he said. 'How are things anyway? Sorry I didn't catch up with you at the funeral. I had my hands full entertaining.'

Cathy stood with her back to him as she waited for the kettle to boil.

'You seem a bit preoccupied yourself. You're surely over your little scare finding the old doctor down the cliffs, aren't you? I'm surprised you stay on here if you're still spooked by it.'

She frowned before turning. 'I'm fine about having found her. A simple suicide, that's what the police said. That's what everyone said. No one in Kinnaven thinks otherwise.'

'Why would they? She was just an old dear who went a bit potty.'

'Exactly. A crazy old doctor with no one to give a shit about if she did jump.'

'If you say so. Why are you getting worked up about it, anyway?'

'Well, no one else is. No one else seems to care.'

Ross put his mug down and came around the counter to her. He wrapped an arm around her waist and turned her to face him. 'You're getting in a bit of a state about this, aren't you?'

He went to kiss her, but she turned away.

'Fine.' He laughed and took a step back. 'You asked me here.' He picked up his mug of tea and walked through to the living room with it.

'Have you been out jogging on the cliffs in the past?' she asked, coming through after him. 'I asked you before if you ever went that way, out onto the moor, and you said no.'

He turned and smiled. 'No, darling, the moor's too dense to run through properly. I stick to the roads to make up the miles and hope not to get run down by motorists like you. I've not been down to the cliffs since I came home at all. The place gives me the creeps.'

Cathy put her mug of tea down on the table and went to the hallway. She fumbled in her jacket pocket and came back through, placing it flat with a snap on the table in front of him.

'The morning of the doctor's death,' she said. 'It caught the light. I saw it immediately.'

Ross picked up the metal disc: an army dog tag with his name, number and blood group engraved onto it. If he was surprised, he didn't show it. He held it out to her.

'You should keep it, sweetheart. We give them out to all the girls. A little keepsake.'

'I think you should go now.'

When he was gone, she wished with all of her heart that she too could leave this place, bundle her clothes and belongings into the back of the car, scribble a note to Jean and Alison, and drop the keys off through the farmhouse door. She'd not have to say goodbye to anyone, she could just up and go. But she knew now that something was very wrong. Ross had been on those cliffs the night that the doctor had died. Why he was involved, she didn't know, but if he had lied to her, she felt sure that more of Kinnaven's residents had been doing so too.

27

'Nothing,' Jean said breathlessly, having obviously run half the way to the cottage. 'I don't have long until I need to get back up the road. Calum's got football training, which is the only reason I managed to get down now, but he's finished in half an hour.'

Cathy beckoned her inside. 'So, you talked to someone today, then? Well done. I thought it would take you longer. Did they think it odd you asking?'

Jean snorted. 'It was that Frances on today, and she's as gossipy as any of them. Fell over herself to tell me what I wanted and probably didn't think twice about doing so.'

Cathy smiled. 'But nothing, you say? Didn't she receive any personal mail this last week or so?'

Jean held up her hand. 'Yes, hang on, I need to get myself straight. When I say nothing, I mean no odd-looking personal things. She did have a couple of bits and pieces, Frances said. One she recognised as being from a trainee she had looked after in her final year. She wrote to Dr Cosgrove from time to time to let her old tutor know how she was getting on, apparently.'

'No, that doesn't sound promising,' Cathy said. 'Anything else?'

'One thing Frances knew for sure was she was sent a personal invite to the big doctors' meeting. That had come with a fancy stamp on the envelope and Dr Cosgrove was chuffed to bits to be asked.'

'The Royal College of General Practitioners,' Cathy said, 'no that's no use either. That rather goes against the idea of suicide though, doesn't it, if she was planning to attend conferences?'

'Hang on. One more, but you'll laugh when I say. The minister.'

Cathy did laugh. 'Well, I hardly think he's in the frame.'

'No, and I even know what the note said because Dr Cosgrove seemingly came out of her room having read it, spitting chips about the contents.'

'My God, what on earth did it say?'

'It was about the minister's group. He's got a band of merry volunteers rounded up and they're ready to oppose any planning applications on the land at Kinnaven Farm. I think the note was giving the doctor a nudge to join them, which I suspect didn't go down too well. I don't for a minute think she approved of the proposed houses, but I suspect she wouldn't have taken kindly to being ordered to attend meetings about it.'

'I suppose I might go up and speak to the minister and find out if he had any idea about her frame of mind before she died.'

'Oh,' Jean said suddenly. 'I forgot completely about that. You only reminded me, talking about her frame of mind. I heard a rumour that Dr Cosgrove had had words with one of the other GPs. Dr Davage, I think. It was about her retirement and whether Dr Cosgrove would still own the practice building. Frances told me about it the other day and it went out of my head. The old doctor was fuming. I'm sorry I forgot. It doesn't give a very convincing motive for murder though, and I can't see one of the doctors killing her partner.'

Cathy raised her eyebrows. 'I suppose people have killed for smaller things. But I agree, it's not quite right. I'm a bit disappointed about the note though, if I'm honest. I guess if we were discussing this with the police, they might have some handwriting expert study the message and tell us for sure who had penned it. I had a bash at copying some of the letters out myself earlier, and I thought I made a pretty good job. I assume whoever did it was trying to hide their real handwriting anyway, and that's why they used capitals.'

Jean looked as if she had failed her friend.

'Oh, don't look like that. It was a bit of a long shot. Perhaps there were no other letters other than this one, or perhaps she received a preceding threat in person. Yes, that might well explain it. That wouldn't narrow the field down at all though.'

'Well, Ross would still be in the frame,' Jean said. 'He could have talked to the doctor while he was at work without any difficulty.'

'True. So could you, and so could I. I went in to see her for a repeat prescription the previous week. Pretty much any of her patients, or just about anyone in Kinnaven itself, could have had a word with her. No, we won't get any further with it in that direction. Don't worry, I've already made a few quiet inquiries of my own in the village. I'm not ready to throw in the towel yet. I want to go up to the farm and speak to Iain or Alison at some point next. They might help me with Ross's movements on the night of the doctor's death if you can't give him an alibi yourself.'

'You know I can't,' Jean said. 'I told you, that was one of the nights he stayed away, along with the night his father died, which to me, does point the finger in his direction.'

Cathy raised an eyebrow. 'Come on, we need something more credible than that. I nearly drove into him when he was out running earlier today. I can't say he was very forthcoming after that.'

Jean snorted. 'Shame you didn't put your foot down and make a good job of it.'

'I assume you and Ross are done?'

'Oh, well and truly,' Jean said. 'I heard you were the mysterious other woman. No secrets in this place.' She laughed. 'Don't be upset. I realise you didn't know about us. It was Ross's fault entirely, not yours. He's played us both.'

'Absolutely nothing happened. Are you okay?'

'I'm fine, actually. Still fuming, of course, but Calum is my priority. Ross would never have settled here long-term, and it's the only place I want to be, so it would never have worked. He'll sell up and go, just you see. That is, unless you can prove he's guilty.'

'You know that's not what I'm doing at all. I'm looking into the deaths, not to pin them on him, but in the hope of finding out the truth. All of it is for the sake of Dr Cosgrove and the old farmer. If no one is to blame, then fine, I can accept that, and so must you. Kinnaven certainly holds some secrets though, doesn't it? How long has the stretch of clifftops been called Devil's Leap, anyway? Has anyone else ever leapt, that you know of?'

Cathy knew instantly that she had hit a raw nerve. Jean's face turned sheet white, and she looked from left to right as if she wanted to be anywhere else. Cathy didn't force the point, and when Jean left not long after, she stood in the empty cottage and smiled. Finally, something had moved. A piece in the puzzle had shown itself. Now, she needed to find how it fitted together.

28

En route to the library, Cathy stopped off at the farmhouse to pay for the following week and to have a quick word with Alison. The late afternoon was clear, but shadows were already lengthening. When she saw the lights were on, butterflies fluttered in her stomach, but for what reason, she couldn't say. She was only paying a bill and hoping to find out about where Ross had been on the night of the doctor's death. Admittedly, this would have to be done with some tact, but it was not really such an onerous task.

A flashy older woman who Cathy remembered seeing at the church and then the pub after the old farmer's funeral opened the door.

'Sorry to intrude,' Cathy said. 'It's perhaps an awkward time?'

The woman held on to the door as if she was going to turn her away, but Alison came out into the hallway.

'Oh, Cathy, come in, come in for goodness' sake. I told Mum to turn anyone away but you're fine.' Alison smiled at the other woman. 'Mum, this is Cathy, the doctor I was telling you about. She's been staying in the lower cottage these last few weeks for a holiday. But it's not turned into much of one, has it, Cathy?'

The older woman stepped back and the front door was opened fully. Cathy walked inside and, seeing the boots and shoes carefully lined at the door and the pristine carpets further in, hastily removed hers.

'Oh, don't be daft, you don't need to bother,' Alison said, and led the way through to the kitchen. 'What a day,' she continued, going over to the door at the far side of the room, opening it and then listening for a moment; she smiled. 'Asleep still, thank God.'

'I'm sorry to come in today. I had wanted to pay before, but the time didn't seem right.' But she was quickly halted by Alison's reaction. The farmer's wife, who had clearly rallied herself since the church service, was shaking her head.

'Cathy helped with Iain's dad when we found him,' she said to her mother. 'Goodness knows what we would have done without her.'

Cathy smiled sardonically. 'I'm afraid it didn't make much of a difference to the outcome though, did it?' She felt as if she was fishing for a compliment and blushed.

'We'd have been lost without you. You don't know how much Iain appreciates what you did,' Alison repeated, and then turning to her mother, went on. 'Poor Cathy found the doctor at the bottom of the cliffs too. What a time you've been having. And Kinnaven was meant to be a break for you from work.'

Cathy shrugged, but feeling embarrassed, she explained her situation, saying that she wanted to stay on a little longer. She found herself embellishing the truth slightly, adding that because she had discovered Dr Cosgrove's body, the police might conceivably still require her in the vicinity to tidy up paperwork.

'Oh, I can quite see,' said Alison. 'They might need you, I

suppose, although it seems pretty straightforward. It seems that the old doctor threw herself off the cliffs,' she explained to her mother. 'The talk around the village was that she was going a bit batty. Nearing retirement, and not quite on-the-ball with her work, so they're saying.'

'Did you know her?' Cathy asked.

'No,' Alison replied. 'I get most of my village gossip from Jean, and she didn't speak too highly.'

'I met her once,' Cathy said. 'I went in for a repeat prescription, just after I'd arrived. I thought she seemed very kind. She didn't rush me out and seemed together.'

Alison smiled. 'She probably knew you were a fellow doctor though, didn't she?'

Cathy assented.

'Yes, I heard she was a bit old-fashioned in her ways. But then, listen to me.' Alison laughed, pressing her hand to her neck. 'I feel sorry for the poor woman, of course. No one deserves an end like that.'

'Dreadful,' said Alison's mum.

Cathy remembered once more what Ross had told her earlier about Alison being found at the top of the cliffs days before the old doctor had jumped herself. He had said that Iain had found her there in the early hours of the morning. She had been standing cold and upset while still holding her baby. Cathy studied Alison's expression and wondered that she wasn't more awkward discussing the events of the last few days. *Just a little too close to home*, Cathy thought to herself. But Alison appeared undeterred from the discussion.

'She must have been in quite a state,' the farmer's wife continued.

'I wonder what made her do it. I mean, why then, just before she was due to retire? And such a shame to do it in such a dramatic way. I must say, it was horrible finding her so close to where I'm staying. The area is too beautiful to imagine something so tragic happening there.'

Alison moved to the door. 'I know. We're lucky to live in this part of the world, but when something like that happens, I suppose it gives the entire community a bit of a stir. It was unfortunate you were out walking and found her.'

'Otherwise, it might have been anyone though,' Cathy persisted. 'You must have plenty of people walking past the end of the road, going for a stroll along the cliffs for the view, with it being so beautiful?'

'Not really,' Alison said, her hand on the door. 'Virtually no one comes down this way. The path is too dangerous and you get a far better view further up the coast. Sorry, Cathy, I'll grab the book, a cheque's fine if you want to do it that way, or just leave it until the end? I think we can trust that you're not going to do a moonlight flit.'

'Dreadful,' Alison's mother repeated as they stood alone waiting for Alison to return.

'Are you staying on yourself?' Cathy asked.

'Me? Oh, no. I came up to help during the funeral and whatnot. Alison was needing an extra pair of hands, I think. I'm going home this afternoon. Perth,' she answered to Cathy's raised eyebrows. 'So not that far.'

'Is he your first grandchild?' Cathy asked.

The woman nodded and smiled. 'First, and the most perfect. I always loved babies,' she said. 'I just wish my husband had been alive to see it happening for Alison. He'd have been proud as punch. We never thought we'd be parents, let alone grandparents, so you can imagine how I'm enjoying things.'

Alison returned, all apologies. 'Cathy, the cottage. I completely forgot. We've got people. Not until the week after, but I'll need you out by the second of the month. Do you think that'll be all right? I can't tell you how sorry I am. I feel like I'm hurrying you on your way.'

'It's fine. Hopefully, things'll be finished by then with the police inquiry or whatever, and I can head home.'

'Alison, if worst comes to the worst, you could put Cathy up in the house. There's the room I'm in,' her mother said.

Cathy thought for a second that she had caught a flash of annoyance in Alison's manner. But the other woman's words soon reassured her.

'Of course, of course. You know you're welcome if you need to stay on. That goes without saying.'

Cathy laughed. 'You've got your hands full with the new baby and Ross staying too. He came down to fix the door hinges the other day. I was very grateful.'

'Oh, Ross is no trouble,' Alison said. 'He's hardly stayed here since he arrived. I'd asked him to go down and check on you the morning after the doctor died, but he was worn out. He said he'd been out half the night with some girlfriend of his in the village. Typical of him. Iain says he was a real tearaway when he was a kid, and I suppose the army hasn't changed him so much.'

Cathy smiled. She thanked Alison and her mother and drove reflectively to the next town, knowing that the previous conversation had revealed another lie and left more questions unanswered.

It only took a couple of minutes to fill out the relevant paperwork to join. She had remembered passing the public library when she had been picking up supplies only the week before. Armed with an ID number to allow her access to the computers, she walked through the building. She found the link to the British Newspaper Database immediately. That was where she would begin. She removed a notepad from her bag but knew that without a date, she had little to go on. She began by narrowing down the search criteria, initially, looking for any deaths reported in the Kinnaven area. This, unfortunately, gave far too many results, and she went back and refined her search to suicides. Again, there were many to choose from, but after ten minutes of trawling the records, reading about a vet who had tragically shot himself and a woman who had thrown herself in front of a train, she specified a time period. She typed in thirty years and found it almost at once.

The newspaper report was of poor literary quality, and the writer chose the most sensational language possible. Cathy scanned through the article once and then read it through again, this time, more slowly. It appeared that an inhabitant of Kinnaven, a twenty-five-year-old woman named Andrea McCabe, had jumped from the cliffs known locally as Devil's Leap in the early hours of 21 August. She had been reported missing along with her child, a three-month-old baby girl, by her husband: Mr John McCabe, a farm labourer. Before a search party had been established, however, their bodies had been discovered by two young boys, out walking the cliffs that morning.

Cathy spent a further hour looking through the records for any follow-up article, and eventually, her efforts were rewarded. It took some time for her heart rate to return to normal and she sat feeling bewildered and horrified at what she had read. Finally, packing away her notepad, she felt sure that she had learned something relevant. It all seemed too coincidental.

It was thirty years ago, to the very day, since the last tragic suicide at Devil's Leap. How awful for a mother to jump, and with her own child in her arms. She still didn't understand the connection with Dr Cosgrove, if indeed there was one. But that wasn't all. It was also thirty years to the day since Jean's brother,

Matthew, had died. The newspaper report had been sketchy but it was there all the same. He had died on the road between Kinnaven and the next town, that very same morning. The morning that the bodies of Andrea McCabe and her baby had been discovered. The report said he had been driving at excessive speed from Kinnaven.

29

The leaves were already beginning to turn. It was too early for autumn, but Cathy felt the change all the same. The greens were fading and becoming yellow. The wind that had struck her getting out of her car at the brow of the hill was all but gone in the churchyard. The old elm trees and the high stone dyke sheltered the place. She entered the small gate and, crossing the path, she moved to the corner of the plot, searching for the grave that she knew must be there. She found it soon enough. 'Matthew Scott 1973–1990' and beneath this inscription, although rubbed and worn over the years: 'Step softly, a dream lies buried here'. Poor Jean and her poor parents, how they must have hurt. Before the grave lay a bunch of flowers. They were past their best. The white petals had begun to wilt and drop.

She heard his steps but did not turn immediately. The shuffle and gentle wheezing cough only proved the owner's identity. She wondered how long they would stand like this, her with her back to him. Eventually, he broke the silence.

'Dr Moreland.'

It was a statement rather than a question, and she thought it odd. How he knew her name, or that she was a doctor, she wasn't sure, but word spread fast in Kinnaven. He had seen her at the old farmer's funeral anyway. Perhaps he considered they were now old acquaintances.

'I hope I didn't startle you,' he said.

'Why should you?' She turned to face him. 'Who else should I expect to find in the churchyard, other than the minister?'

He bowed his head in acknowledgement and offered his arm, a peculiar gesture, given that, due to his frailty, she should have been the one offering hers. Feeling slightly repelled but not knowing why, she touched the black material of his sleeve, and together they walked the path to the church in silence. Cathy glanced from side to side as they walked, noting the other flowers that had been left. And then, as they rounded the corner of the church, she saw the mound of fresh earth, heaped with floral tributes on the old farmer's recently settled grave. The minister paused, slightly breathless and following her gaze, nodded.

'You didn't stay for the full service.'

'No,' Cathy agreed. 'I'm more interested in the living than the dead.' But she immediately regretted her words.

'Indeed, doctor?' he mocked. 'That is not, if you don't mind me saying, what I had heard. But then Kinnaven can be such a strange village. I suspect that many Scottish hamlets are much the same.' He dropped her arm and walked more freely ahead as they entered the church. He held the door wide and then closed it firmly behind them.

Uneven ground, Cathy thought. That was where he was unbalanced. As soon as he was on the level stone of the church, he was like a different person. The wind outside blustered around the corner of the old building and Cathy heard it catching at the high branches of the trees outside. She shivered and held the folds of her jacket tightly around her.

'Nearly upon us,' the minister said, almost in understanding, and then, in explanation, 'Autumn.' He turned, as if addressing the empty church, his voice raised: '*A wind has blown the rain and blown the sky and all the leaves away, but the trees stand. I think I, too, have known autumn too long.*' He smiled at her. 'Cummings, I think. A lesser-known American poet.'

Cathy felt a mildly hysterical giggle rise in her.

The minister was now looking at her acutely. His eyes, although aged and clouded, were bright and his manner was strangely earnest.

'I had come to look...' Cathy began.

'Come, come. We are friends, are we not, doctor?'

'But it's true. I heard about Jean's brother, Matthew. I needed to see for myself.'

The minister shook his head sadly and lowered himself into the first pew, turning awkwardly to face her. 'I saw you with her and the mother at the funeral. Trouble.' He looked hard at her. 'Oh, dear. But I only speak the truth. The whole family. Pagans!'

'But she cleans for you, doesn't she?'

'An offer of hope,' he said, his voice echoing unhappily. 'Years ago, I made a proposal and how have I been repaid?'

'Well, presumably she's cleaned for you and has done a good job if her work on my rental cottage is anything to go by.'

The minister chuckled. 'Yes, you are right in what you say. In literal terms, she has fulfilled her end of the bargain perfectly. But I meant that I had offered her something more, as I think you understand only too well. I had offered her amnesty, even mercy.'

'From what?'

'Poor Jeanie Scott.' His voice was melodic. 'She was a lost child in many ways, and particularly so when her brother died. Her mother is the one at fault. No morals.'

Cathy was shocked by his hostility, the way he almost spat his words out, but he seemed not to notice.

'I offered Jean a chance to reform and to improve herself. She shacked up with every other man in the village at one time or another until poor unfortunate Daniel came along and became ensnared. And then, even he was cast aside. I hear she's taken up with another one recently and he is far worse than the rest. I offered her my home and the church as a safe haven...'

'But where God built a church, the devil also built a chapel?' Cathy asked and then smiled at the minister's surprise.

'Martin Luther? Yes, I see that you understand only too well. A thief and a liar, I am afraid. She continues to clean for me and will do so for as long as she chooses. Things have gone missing but I turn a blind eye. We have an understanding now. I live in hope that she will change, but for now...'

'I don't understand.'

'Why I'm saying this and to you of all people? A warning,' the minister said. 'In you, dear child, please don't be offended in me saying this, but in you, I see a lost soul also, just like young Jeanie Scott. I saw it as soon as we met at the funeral. How little it would take for you also to go down that same road.'

Cathy recoiled at his words. 'I'm hardly going to steal!'

'No?' asked the minister, and the question hung in the air.

Cathy found herself unable to answer and wondered even if she blushed, thinking of the morphine sulphate she had taken from work.

'Perhaps you have already.' Raising himself from the seat, he began to walk down the church aisle, his footsteps echoing off the stone walls. Cathy watched his stooped figure, bathed in the emerald greens, the unfathomable blues and then, blood reds of the stained-glass window.

'You are in too deep, doctor.' His voice drifted back to her as cold as the stone itself. 'I think you know very well of what I speak, and believe me, I would not say it otherwise. I feel I must urge you to leave our hamlet now and to make haste in doing so.

I am an old man, but of this I am sure. Go now, before anything evil can touch you. Kinnaven, in many ways, seems to bring it out in people, and, from what I have observed, you have no strength to fight.'

Cathy left him there. As she turned, he seemed almost to wither and fade like the flowers that lay on the graves outside. She paused with her hand on the door, wondering for a moment if the man, so strange and eccentric in his manner, had locked her in. But the door opened wide and a gust of wind blew into the chapel. She turned again, seeing his stooped figure now blind to her existence.

Picking her way back to the car, she paused as she passed Matthew Scott's grave. Poor Matty. She felt sure that the boy's death was linked to that of the doctor, but how? She couldn't ask Jean or her mother, and the minister was completely out of the question now. She wondered at the old man's sanity after their conversation and was glad to be away. But still, why had Jean's brother been driving from Kinnaven that night of all nights? Cathy thought of the other tragedy that dreadful day thirty years before and wondered if Matthew had known the woman and child who had died. What could have possibly driven the desperate young mother to do such a thing? Impulsively, having already settled herself in her car and turned on the engine, she unclipped her seat belt and went out once more into the howling wind.

In truth, she thought, this was why she had come to the churchyard in the first place. She found the grave almost immediately, marked by two fresh, white roses. In bygone days, burial on consecrated ground was forbidden in the case of a suicide. Thank goodness, Kinnaven had not been so unforgiving. It was at the other side of the path from Matty's grave and had a simpler tombstone. She wondered if it was common practice to bury a mother and her child together, even if the mother had murdered the baby. Infanticide was very rare, thank God, and she had never come across a case in her career, but she knew that if a mother did kill her child, then she invariably killed herself at the same time.

She read the inscription, parting the grasses that grew tall, obscuring the final line. Who, she wondered, had placed the flowers there so recently?

'Andrea and Amy McCabe,' the engraving read, and then their dates of birth, and, of course, the same date of death. Andrea had been only twenty-five, and the baby only three months old. 'Unable are the loved to die, for love is immortality,' she read.

This time Cathy did not hear the footsteps behind her. Nor did she hear the swing of the branch as it crashed down upon her fragile skull.

30

'What a bloody carry-on. Nearly died getting up here. Flashed by a speed camera too, so that'll be another three points. Jesus, you know how to scare someone.'

When Suzalinna finally stopped fighting her way out of her jacket, she bent down and gently hugged her friend. 'Don't bloody scare me like that again,' she said. 'What a dump of a hospital, no? Not how I remember it at all. Like going back in time, isn't it? Do they know you're a medic or are we keeping quiet about that?'

Cathy laughed but her head throbbed. 'I didn't know I was a medic until yesterday. I could barely tell you my own name. Are we getting out of here soon? I heard them saying they were getting pharmacy to send up my meds, but that was ages ago now.'

She almost wished she hadn't asked because her friend began clicking her fingers at every passing nurse, a gesture which was ignored until, finally, Suzalinna got up and stalked from the room. Cathy sighed as she overheard her asking if she could speak to the registrar on call for the ward.

When Suzalinna eventually returned, she had positive news.

'I just spoke to him and it's on its way. Pharmacy got a kick up the butt. The registrar went to med school the same year as us – Edinburgh graduate. Dallied in general surgery and then had a rethink. I told him he should've had a crack at A&E but he said he was too squeamish.'

Cathy smiled. 'You'll be inviting him round for dinner next. How's Saj? Is he furious?'

'Don't be ridiculous. Saj doesn't possess such emotion. No, he's fine. Work was fine too. I was off yesterday and today anyway, and Brodie said he'd do my on calls if I wasn't back soon enough. Saj was worried about you, of course, as we all were when the police phoned. Thank God you had my name under your emergency contact number and I could tell them about the antipsychotics.'

'Oh my God.' Cathy sat forward. Her head thumped.

'Calm down. You've had the correct dose. Nothing bad will come of this. Once we collect your discharge scrip, we'll cut and run. I take it that's the plan? We'll sort out your car and collect it in a few weeks, maybe. Saj can catch the train up and drive it back for you.'

'I hadn't thought. I need to go back to the cottage.'

'Of course. We'll get your things sorted. That's fine. You can even say your goodbyes or whatever, and we'll pay up and head this evening. I prefer night-driving, anyway. Roads'll be empty.'

A sense of unease fell over Cathy. Over the last day, as her memories had fully returned, she had thought a good deal about the events over the past few weeks. The minster found her on the ground beside a big elm branch. They assumed that it had snapped from the tree in an unusually strong gust of wind, falling directly onto her, and knocking her out. Cathy wasn't so sure. Another accident like the doctor's death, and yet again, it had been so conveniently accepted by Kinnaven's residents. But still, there were questions to be answered. Her head pulsated with any movement and instinctively she reached out a hand to touch at the wound.

'Leave the head,' Suzalinna said, without even looking at her. Cathy glanced sideways and saw her friend grinning. It was good to see her – really good.

'God knows how you get yourself into these situations,' Suzalinna scolded. 'I hear your practice has found a long-term locum now. They'll be delighted to see you back though, even if it's just for a coffee when you're able. You look quite different, you know? The tablets have clearly helped. I still can't believe all this though,' she gestured to the bed.

Cathy shrugged. Maybe it was the bump to the head. Perhaps it was that she had more pressing things to think about. She remembered the gravestone again. She remembered kneeling to look at the words. Cathy had played and replayed the moments before she blacked out. How was the doctor's death connected to a tragedy thirty years before? Why would anyone in Kinnaven remember, let alone want to hush it up? And why would they want her to stop asking questions? Cathy felt sure of one thing: someone in Kinnaven wanted her quietened. They wanted her to go back to where she had come from, to stop talking about Angela and Amy McCabe, to stop querying the doctor's supposed suicide and the farmer's death. Cathy knew without a doubt that she had been deliberately struck on the head. Dispassionately, as she sat on the hospital bed with her friend beside her, she knew that she was in danger staying on in Kinnaven. But she also knew that this was what she must do.

As she sat there in the hospital with Suzalinna by her side, Cathy thought of her consultation with Dr Cosgrove. She considered the doctor, so close to retirement and in the village she had loved and served for so long. How could they all move on, accepting her death so easily? Dr Cosgrove might well have been a cold and austere type but she was an unbiased doctor. Fair and knowledgeable. Cathy considered her own patients. Would they mourn her if she didn't return to them? She hoped they might. She turned to Suzalinna, who was fidgeting with her enormous bag, rummaging to find something or other at the bottom of it.

'I'm not coming back,' Cathy said. 'I need to stay in Kinnaven and finish what I've started.'

31

Cathy left Suzalinna stewing in the cottage and hesitantly made her way across the moor. She knew her friend was livid. She had messed up her plans to return home and had been unusually obstinate. Suzalinna was almost always the driving force in any decision. Cathy would ordinarily go along with what she said to keep the peace, but not today.

It took her twenty minutes to pick her way across the heathery land to the house. What kind of person would choose to live here alone? Someone who had actively chosen to take themselves away from the company of others and any modern conveniences or comforts.

'So, you've come, have you?' he asked.

'I'm sorry to bother you. Can I come in?'

He opened the door wider, allowing her past, and waved her to the right with a hand still holding a lit cigarette. The house had not seen a visitor in many years. The wallpaper in the hallway was peeling, and the heavily patterned carpet had not been swept in a long time. A camp chair sat against the wall. She had seen him using it the other day.

'You'll have to clear a place to sit,' he challenged. 'I don't get visitors.'

She would have preferred not to sit. The room was basic to the extreme. Two ancient armchairs were positioned by a wood-burner, the nearest was covered by a tartan blanket and the other was piled high with clothes. A haze of nicotine hung in the fabric of the place. She transferred some clothes to the arm of the chair and sat. The back of her head throbbed with the change of position.

Looking up, she saw that the walls were covered with canvases. The room had been so dimly lit that it had taken her this long to notice. They were all the same scene, the clifftops at Kinnaven, but all were entirely different. One, in particular, was mesmerising. An eerie balance of light and shade. Such a simple composition, but painted so originally.

He watched her for a moment or two and slowly seated himself in the other chair. 'Well, then. I hope this isn't to discuss my painting again. You know very little about art.'

She laughed. 'You're right about that. No. It's just that I am leaving Kinnaven soon. I've stayed long enough to witness a sudden death and an apparent suicide, which I can't for the life of me understand. Kinnaven has certainly left its mark.' Her head pulsated once more.

The man said nothing, but blinked slowly.

'I felt I couldn't go without speaking to you again. I'm a doctor, you see?'

He drew heavily on the end of his cigarette and stubbed it out deliberately on the table beside him. Leaning back in his chair, he clasped his hands. His knuckles were ossified calluses. 'So, you've come to tell me I'm dying, have you? You needn't bother. I know that much without the aid of a medical degree, thank you.'

'Have you seen a doctor?'

He snorted and was then paralysed by a fit of coughing that wracked through his whole body. 'No, I haven't seen a doctor. Not in over thirty years. That shocks you, does it?' He smiled, but his eyes remained cold. 'So, what gave my diagnosis away, may I ask?'

'Your hands. You have what is medically referred to as finger clubbing. The nails bend over, you see?' She gestured, making a semicircle with her forefinger. 'It can happen for many reasons, but judging by the nicotine stains on your fingers, I thought that lung cancer was the probable cause. I'm sorry.'

He smiled bitterly at her. 'A wonderful piece of deduction. You must be an excellent doctor. Your patients should count themselves fortunate. But it's of no interest to me. I am beyond that.' He smiled and spoke in almost a whisper. 'I have been waiting for it. Waiting all these years.'

'Waiting? I don't understand. Waiting for what?'

'For death. Oh, don't look so horrified. This life has had little pleasure for me other than my art. And now the end is near, my work has blossomed.'

'Have you any family? Children? Relatives? Don't you want to let them know?'

He slowly turned to face her. 'What did you say your name was?'

'Cathy. Cathy Moreland.'

'Well, Dr Moreland. I must thank you for your house call, but if you'll excuse me, I have work to be getting on with. You won't mind seeing yourself out, I'm sure.'

'So, are you going to talk to me then, or have I come all this way to sit and look at you? Seriously, Cathy, I thought you'd want to be on your way. I thought you'd be desperate to get out of this bloody place. I know we talked about a holiday but it's not been much of one. Granted, you've done admirably, taking your tablets like a good girl, but really? What's the big reason to stay on? Oh, and what were you talking to that doctor at the hospital about? Whispering away like there was some big secret. I hate not knowing, just let me in.'

She had been sitting staring blankly at the television screen for the past twenty minutes. Still, it made no sense.

'What?' she asked, further infuriating Suzalinna, who got up and stalked through to the bedroom. Cathy could hear her phoning Saj.

Who had left the flowers on the grave? Who was mourning Angela and Amy still after all these years? More to the point, what did it have to do with the two deaths? Cathy felt more content about the farmer's death now, but it was not coincidental that the doctor had died on the very day that, thirty years before, the poor mother and child had perished.

She was roused from her ponderings by a knock on the door. Before she could rise to answer, it was opened and she heard someone wiping their feet hurriedly on the doormat. Cathy got up.

'Jesus Christ! Well, you gave us all a scare. Thank God you're all right.' Jean was already taking off her ankle boots and lining them neatly at the edge of the carpet.

Cathy smiled. She hadn't seen her friend since the day of the accident. She remembered the old minister's warning about her family. It seemed inconceivable to believe that Jean was anything other than kind and honest as she stood in the hallway. Cathy was again reminded of her initial impression of Jean, and despite the things she kept hearing about her, that stubbornly remained the same.

'Come on through,' she said. 'You heard about my little accident then?' She turned around and parting the hair carefully on the back of her head, she bent down so Jean could see.

'Bloody hell! Got you good and proper.'

'Stung a bit.' Cathy laughed and, walking through to the kitchen, she began to take mugs from the cupboard.

'Alison told me to leave doing the cottage, but I couldn't. I knew you'd be back and I wanted a chat.' Without thinking, Jean scooped some crumbs from the counter into her palm and then tipped them into the sink.

'Have you seen the minister?'

'He found you, I hear. Yes, I was up there cleaning the other day and he told me all about it. What a sad case he is. Seems half-mad with loneliness creaking around that old manse. Goodness knows what he does with himself. Gives me the creeps sometimes. All he does is read when I'm there, but what a mess it always is. Not my favourite job for sure.'

Suzalinna appeared in the kitchen doorway. 'Oh hello?' she said in surprise. She still held her mobile phone. 'Rubbish reception,' she explained. 'I'm just nipping out and seeing if it's better around the front of the house. Saj says hi, by the way.'

Cathy heard her friend putting on a jacket and going outside, closing the front door with a bang. Jean looked questioningly.

'My old friend from university,' Cathy said. 'She drove up when she heard about the accident. She's meant to be driving us home again. I think she's getting impatient with me.'

Jean laughed. 'So, what are your plans then? Are the doctors from the hospital happy for you to travel? And what about the deaths? I don't expect you to look into it any further now.'

Before she could answer there was a thumping of shoes and Suzalinna came into the kitchen once more, but this time looking windswept. 'Can't get a bloody signal anywhere,' she said. Then, she followed Jean's gaze down to the floor and the muddy footprints she had just walked through the house; Suzalinna grimaced. Cathy saw the trail of dirt scattered across the beige carpet.

'Idiot,' Cathy said and Suzalinna hurriedly removed her shoes.

'It's fine, it's fine,' Jean said. 'I told you before, it happens. No, don't wet it further, Cathy, you'll make it worse. Let me get at it.'

Jean picked the worst offending cakes of mud by hand.

'Sorry,' Suzalinna mouthed.

'Honestly, it's nothing,' Jean said. 'Up the road, that's where they're worst for it. Last time I was livid. Usually, I don't mind. It's par for the course, really. But last time, that was when I wanted to get down to you quick. Remember when you had your fright over finding the doctor down those cliffs? Sick with worry about you, I was. But mud everywhere that morning, and all over the boots, although goodness knows where they'd had been, and early in the morning too. Wet mud, caked right through, nearly to the kitchen, it was. What a mess. This is nothing in comparison.' Jean looked up. 'What? What have I said?'

Cathy had placed her mug of tea down on the worktop.

'Cathy?' Suzalinna asked and moved towards her. 'Cathy? Are you going to faint? What is it?'

She looked at them blankly.

'I think I know who,' she said to the room. Then, composing herself: 'Jean, I need you to help me. I need you to do me a massive favour.'

32

Cathy had met so many of Kinnaven's residents over the past few weeks, but so far, she and Jean's mother had only spoken briefly at the old farmer's funeral. Perhaps if they had talked more, the entire mystery might have been concluded sooner. Mary, Jean's mother, required little encouragement. Even with Jean and Suzalinna sitting there in the woman's small living room, she wasn't put off. If anything, she seemed to enjoy the attention. She needed to tell her story. She had waited too long.

'It's good of you to see us,' Cathy began.

Jean's mother nodded and smiled. 'Well then, what do you want from me?'

'Well, I'm convinced that Dr Cosgrove's death is not unrelated to another death. But it was many years ago. Thirty, to be exact. I still can't work out the real connection. Maybe you can help with that? Perhaps you can remember? Well, I know you will.' Cathy glanced at Jean and saw the other woman looking down at her hands. 'I understand that it's difficult. Jean didn't want to, you see?'

'I remember the night only too well. It's as if it was yesterday,' Jean's mother said. 'It's rarely spoken about, not now. That was the night that the McCabe woman threw herself over the cliffs with her baby. That's what you mean, isn't it? He hates it when it's mentioned.' Jean's mother nodded to the door, indicating that she meant her husband. 'Why you're so odd about it, Jeanie, I can't understand. It was a tragedy, yes, but like so many Scottish coastal villages, we have our tales. It's well known about the place. People avoid going there. Devil's Leap, I mean. I think the stories started long before then anyway. When my mother was a girl, she wasn't allowed down either.'

Cathy nodded. 'I got a sense of it myself. I heard about the McCabe tragedy, but it was a tragic night for other reasons too... The night that your son died also.'

Cathy watched as Mary turned to her daughter. Jean refused to look up, but her mother nodded sadly.

'It must still hurt. I'm so sorry,' said Cathy. 'Can you tell me about it? Please take your time. I'm in no rush.'

Jean's mother leant back in her chair and closed her eyes for a moment. It was as if she was transporting herself back. Back to a night which must have changed her whole family forever, but also many more in the process.

'I suppose I should start at the beginning,' Mary finally said, having composed herself. 'Our part in it is minor really and comes towards the end.' Jean snorted, but her mother went on. 'Jean must have been only four or five at the time. She'll not remember much, I imagine. Back then, the village wasn't so different from how it is now. Small-minded folk and gossip, rife about nothing much. I don't remember the McCabes being part of village life, though. They lived some way out and I suppose they kept themselves to themselves, although the husband seemed to be at the pub a good deal, I believe. Bit of a loner and that probably didn't help when things went so badly wrong. I think after the tragedy of him losing his wife and baby, folk did try to reach out to him, but he was a lost cause.

Drowned his sorrows and then left the place for good. I don't blame him. How could you stay on living here after that? There was a lot of talk at the time about the doctor. This was going way back, mind. There always is talk about doctors in small villages like this,' Mary said with a smile. 'We blame them for everything and rarely remember to say thank you when they do get things right. Even recently, that Mrs Brice from next door had been saying that the surgery's going downhill, forgetting about their elderly patients and not doing enough house calls, or some such nonsense. But you can't please everyone, can you?'

Cathy agreed that you could not.

'Back then, there was a lot of gossip going around. A lot of bad feeling generally, and then, after the McCabes, it seemed to escalate. The family, as I say, upped and left soon after, though.'

'What were the people saying about the deaths?' Cathy asked.

'Oh, the usual. Blaming. They always need to blame someone, don't they, after something like that happens? But she was cleared of any negligence or wrong-doing at the time. I remember it well.'

'Dr Cosgrove, you mean? But why did they blame her?'

'They said that she missed the fact that Mrs McCabe was suicidal. Apparently, the young mother had been in twice to see her at the surgery. They said she was begging for help, saying she was depressed or whatever. But they said that Dr Cosgrove wasn't interested. Nonsense really, but it's what they said.'

'But why?'

'That,' said Jean's mum, 'is small villages for you. But once something like that starts up, it spreads. Poor Dr Cosgrove had a rough few years of it, I think. Surprised she didn't throw in the towel and start up elsewhere. Perhaps that's why I didn't mind her so much myself. Fighting spirit, like me,' she chuckled.

'I suppose it must have shaken the place up a good deal,' said Cathy.

'It did. And then there was the way the bodies were found, and our own heartbreak,' she continued, turning to her daughter. Jean's eyebrows knitted.

'Oh?' asked Cathy.

'Hasn't Jean told you any of this?' asked her mother. And when Cathy shook her head, Mary continued, sighing first and resettling herself in her seat. 'I'll never forget that night. None of our family could. God knows it nearly killed me, but we had folk about us, not like the McCabes. We spoke about Matty. It was hard at first, of course, but we didn't want him to be forgotten. We: me and Jean's dad, wanted to remember him, to speak of him often, even if it hurt. We still do, but those early days...' The woman looked skyward and her eyes glistened. 'Oh, those early days, I felt I might go half-mad with the pain. No one can explain to you the hurt of losing a child. It's physical,' she said, and clenched her fist to her heart. 'Right here,' she said. 'Ploughed into, in the early hours of that morning. He shouldn't have been out, but that's boys for you. It wasn't his fault. A police car,' she said, now looking down at her hands. She turned her wedding ring around and around her finger.

Cathy shifted uncomfortably. She had read the newspaper article in the library and, although the report had been sketchy, this had been mentioned.

'Hurtling down the coastal road to get to the newly found McCabes, who'd just been discovered at the bottom of the cliffs by two kids. The car, the police car, crashed head-on into our boy's motorbike. I'll never forgive myself for allowing him to have the damn machine, but he'd passed his test and was so proud. Instantaneous, thank God. They said he wouldn't have suffered.' Although it was difficult to go on, she forced herself. 'Jean was our saviour in those early days,' she said. 'She didn't understand, being so young. Looked up to her big brother though and kept asking when he'd be home.'

Cathy looked across at Jean, who sat stony-faced.

'I didn't understand the link between the two tragedies,' Cathy said apologetically. 'Of course, the police car had been going to the cliffs, and en route hit poor Matty...'

Mary's hands twisted in her lap.

'You said that the McCabes' bodies were found by children?' Cathy asked, still trying to piece the thing together.

'What a time it was for the village.' Jean's mother nodded. 'Blue lights and sirens going on for what seemed like forever. Yes, they were discovered by children. I've often wondered what effect it's had on them. One of them coming back here to settle with his new wife and the youngest, such dear friends always with you, Jean.'

Cathy felt panic rise in her throat. 'Hold on, Mary, let me get this straight. I might not be understanding you right. Are you saying what I think you're saying?'

Mary raised her eyebrows in puzzlement. 'The old farmer's boys. Yes. That's who found the bodies. Been out monkeying around early that morning. Said they were looking for a cave down by Devil's Leap. A lot of nonsense. There's never been a cave down there, and I've lived here all my life, so you'd think I'd know.'

'Iain and Ross? They found Andrea and her baby, dead at the bottom of the cliffs that day, thirty years ago?'

'Yes,' said the woman with mild exasperation. 'Although they didn't climb down, obviously. The men had to get ropes and all sorts to winch them up.' Mary shuddered. 'Awful business, it was. Devil's Leap. Never liked that name.'

Bile rose in Cathy's throat. Sick at the thought of Iain and Ross, as young children, seeing such a dreadful thing. How must it have shaped their lives since? Perhaps it went some way to explaining Ross's changeable demeanour.

'I think we've troubled you enough,' she said, seeing the woman sigh heavily. Suzalinna and Jean got up, and they made their way to the door.

'I'll be in later, Mum,' Jean called back, and Mary blew her a kiss. 'Don't brood, now,' Jean said and then smiled as she heard her mother's indignant answer.

'Well, what now?' asked Suzalinna as they stood in front of the house.

'I'm sorry, Jean,' Cathy said, ignoring her friend's question. 'Sorry about your brother. Sorry about everything.'

Jean shrugged. 'It was a long time ago, but things like that aren't easily forgotten. Nearly crazy with it, they were. Mum especially.'

'Thanks for allowing us to hear your story. I can see why you didn't want to talk about it yourself,' Cathy said, and for the second time that day, her face went pale. Suzalinna stepped forward and grabbed her arm.

'Steady, Cath. I think you're needing a lie-down, darling. You fractured your skull only a few days ago, and I think all of this has been too much.'

Suzalinna was quite right, and Cathy allowed herself to be guided down to the farm cottage once more, but only after she had returned to Jean's mother to ask one last question.

Finally, it all made sense.

33

'I'll never know if it was deliberate. If you actively lured her there and then pushed her over the edge,' Cathy said. 'No one will know, certainly not the police, given their apparent disinterest. I suspect she popped in on the way home from work that night. Perhaps she came to apologise, or to make some kind of amends, having finally realised who you were.' Cathy sighed and surveyed the room. No one moved. 'You'd seen her several times in the street and maybe even in the surgery. Perhaps you dared to mention the long-forgotten tragedy. Maybe you tested to see how she would react.'

Cathy paused and nodded. 'Yes. I think that's how it was. Dr Cosgrove must have been utterly horrified to have it brought up again, having tried so hard to forget. And then, when she realised who you were, it must have been excruciating for her.' Cathy raised her hand and touched the back of her head. It throbbed with predictable discomfort. 'The saddest thing,' she went on, 'is that the old doctor had already decided. She went to Devil's Leap with the full intention of killing herself. Your hand was not necessary, not in the least. But whether you manhandled her or not, we'll never know. Either way, in my eyes, you are entirely responsible for her death. Those vindictive notes, and then, her appointment with death... It was horribly cruel.'

She looked around at the room again, at all of their faces now, watching and listening, hanging on her every word. Suzalinna was by her side, seated at the table, ready to jump to her aid if required.

On returning to the cottage from Jean's mother, Cathy had slept for four hours straight and had only then felt ready. The excitement had been too much, and she knew she needed to gather herself. Her dreams had been filled with the usual horrors of falling, but she was no longer frightened. What she must do was inevitable. Kinnaven and its residents had suffered long enough. It had to end. When she woke, Suzalinna had already begun to pack the car.

'One final thing,' she had told her friend. 'I have to do one more thing.'

Suzalinna hadn't questioned her this time.

Now, in the farmhouse kitchen, Jean stood awkwardly, her back pressed up against the pine dresser. Cathy had called and begged her to meet them there, telling her they were leaving that afternoon and wanted to say goodbye. Jean had been a bit funny on the phone, especially when Cathy asked her to bring her mother too, but she must have realised that it was important.

Alison moved around the granite island now, holding her baby, still sleeping in her arms. She had already played host magnificently and had rallied, producing a full teapot and biscuit barrel. Cathy smiled at her. She had only told her that she was coming to pay and then planned to head home. The look of surprise on the poor woman's face when near-enough half of Kinnaven, not to mention the minister, had appeared at her front door.

The minister had been somewhat trickier to convince. He had been busy writing a sermon for Sunday's service when she called. Cathy had all but begged for his co-operation, finally intimating that she now knew who had hit her over the head with a branch in his churchyard. The minister had been scandalised, saying that he thought she had made some kind of mistake, but he had come to the farmhouse all the same.

Iain and Ross looked uncomfortable as they stood by the back door, the only place left for them, given that the minister was seated at the table with Suzalinna and Jean's mum. Ross, in particular, couldn't meet her or Jean's gaze, and Cathy knew that as she spoke, she was blushing again.

'If you have no proof,' Iain suddenly said, 'then how do you expect us to believe any of this? And why would any of us want Dr Cosgrove dead?'

Cathy turned to him. 'It's rather close to home, Iain. I'm sorry to bring it up at all, but I knew after I was hit on the back of the head that someone in Kinnaven was desperate. It took me an eternity to work out why.' Cathy shook her head wistfully. 'It started thirty years ago, when a young mother, not much older than you, Alison, visited the doctor suffering from postnatal depression. For whatever reason, Dr Cosgrove didn't recognise the signs. I believe myself, that she was a good and hard-working woman. Perhaps she had an off-day. Of course, that's no excuse. Her error of judgement led to a catalogue of catastrophes. Jean and Mary?' Cathy turned to the two women. 'Of course, by chance, it impacted your lives too. Ultimately,' she said to the rest of the room, 'by missing the diagnosis of severe postnatal depression, it led to Andrea McCabe, that poor young woman, throwing herself from the cliffs. It was a tragedy in itself but she took with her, her child, a three-month-old baby girl called Amy.'

Alison gasped and covered her mouth with her hand. Iain

went to her and they looked down at their own son. 'It's horrible,' she whispered. 'Horrible.'

'It was you that found them, Iain and Ross. I'm so sorry about that. It must have been dreadful and something that will stay with you all your lives.'

Alison turned on Iain. 'What? You never said! How can it have been you?'

'It was a long time ago when we were just kids,' he said. 'All but forgotten.'

'Long ago, but certainly *not* forgotten,' the minister said gravely.

Cathy nodded. 'No. Not forgotten. But it wasn't the only tragedy caused that day, as I've already said. Poor Matty Scott, who was driving out of Kinnaven that morning, also fell victim to a set of uncontrollable, almost inconceivable, circumstances. He was mown down by one of the police cars as it sped towards the scene.'

'So, you're saying that Dr Cosgrove inadvertently caused three deaths?' asked Ross.

'Exactly,' Cathy said. 'Not to mention, shaping the lives of all those concerned. That includes you and your brother, Ross.'

This time, it was Ross's turn to redden, but Cathy continued. She was on a roll and nothing could have stopped her.

'I suppose I made the connection when I was in the churchyard that day, minister. You'll remember our little chat? I had gone to look at Matthew Scott's grave, but I saw the other memorial while I was there. The grave of the mother and child. I also noticed the flowers placed there. Two white roses. It was a foolish thing to do, in the circumstances, and it made me wonder who had left such a tribute. I might never have believed that anyone in Kinnaven still remembered but, of course, someone did, only too well.' Cathy glanced to the minister. 'You knew that there was something malevolent in your village. I think you channelled your ill-feeling towards the proposed property developers, assuming that any change to the place might spell its downfall. You even accused Jean of being immoral, feeling that the spite had originated from her. You had a strong impression that something was wrong. You tried to warn me before I was knocked on the head.' Cathy spread her hands wide and grinned. 'I was rather asking for that, I suppose, but it confirmed that someone didn't want me poking around. A warning. Not to kill me, but to give me a bloody good scare.'

'You could have easily died,' Suzalinna said, angrily. 'A hairline skull fracture!'

'I don't think that was intentional, although maybe I'm wrong.'

No one spoke. Expectancy hung in the air. Finally, it seemed that Jean could bear it no longer. 'I'm sorry to ask, but you've only spoken about Dr Cosgrove. There was another death in question also.'

'Iain and Ross's father? Yes. I thought about that a good deal, truly I did. Indeed, he might have been poisoned with digoxin. I know from speaking to Alison earlier, that he took it for an arrhythmia. It might have been quite easy to incrementally increase his dose and kill him that way. A heart attack would be his cause of death, and without a post-mortem, no one would think anything untoward had occurred.'

'Well then?' Jean asked.

Cathy shook her head and smiled. 'I happened to speak to one of the doctors at the hospital while I was getting my head patched up. I told him that I had been involved in the man's resuscitation. He remembered the farmer, having seen him in A&E. He was forced to call an end to the heroics in resus. They got him back briefly, but the ECG showed no reverse tick waves.' Cathy looked at Suzalinna.

'No digoxin toxicity then,' her friend said.

'Exactly. No, Jean, however much you might have convinced yourself of it, there was no crime. No overdose, no poisoning. His cardiac enzymes: a blood level routinely measured when someone comes into A&E with a cardiac arrest, showed he had had a massive myocardial infarction. He died of natural causes and Ross and Iain benefit justly.'

Ross shot a look of anger at Jean.

'Going back to the doctor's death though, which as I've said, worried me from the start... Jean, you gave it away down in the cottage earlier, as it happens. You have been such a dear friend to me since I arrived. Both you and your mother have been so kind. You, especially, welcomed me unconditionally since I came to Kinnaven. I've had my own demons to deal with, as I'm sure you know only too well. But you have been nothing but generous.'

Jean took a step forward. 'What? What is it you're saying? That I...?'

But Suzalinna was standing now, and even Ross had begun to edge forward. Cathy smiled across at him, and for the first time since the awkwardness that day in the cottage over the metal dog tag she had found on the moors, there was an understanding.

'It's all right,' she said. 'I know it wasn't you who pushed the doctor over the edge, Jean. Don't be utterly ridiculous. I did wonder though when I found Ross's dog tag there that morning. I thought, of course, that it was him who had dropped it, but realised quickly that he must surely have owned several and given one to you when he left for the army, all but a boy, fifteen years ago. You kept yours, of course, despite marrying another man, knowing that your young heart was Ross's forever. Ross had seen you through a painful childhood, haunted and overwhelmed by grief. I think, given your recent relations with Ross, you found the dog tag once more, perhaps having forgotten it, and began wearing it again. It was you who accidentally dropped it on the way to my cottage the previous day when you were cleaning, not Ross at all, that night.'

Jean blushed.

'No, the dog tag was a red herring. Discovering it confused me, but I should thank you for leading me to who *was* responsible for the doctor's death. You see, Andrea McCabe, on killing herself and her baby daughter, left a family behind. There was, of course, her husband. He was broken by the death of his wife and child. But there was also another young daughter. It was Mary, Jean's mother, who confirmed this, but I suppose I had an idea. The two of them, the father and daughter, apparently fled Kinnaven not long after the tragedy, unable to bear living in a place that held so many dreadful memories.'

Jean relaxed a little but continued to smile a little nervously.

'Jean, you made me think. It was down at the cottage. Do you remember? Suzalinna, my friend here from university, never did think about anyone other than herself, even when we were training to be doctors. Brilliant, but arrogant, isn't that right, Suz?'

Suzalinna shifted uncomfortably but didn't speak.

'It's always been the same with you, hasn't it, Suzalinna? You've always spoken before considering the consequences, always crashed right in without thinking?'

'Bloody character assassination,' Suzalinna said quietly.

'In the cottage, you did just that though, didn't you? You came stomping in, having tried to make a call to Saj outside because you said the reception was bad in the house. Came crashing in through the house carrying mud and muck on your boots for poor Jean to clear up.'

Everyone looked puzzled.

'And then, Jean,' Cathy said. 'You said it to me, then and

there, when you were cleaning up the mud, do you remember?'

Jean shook her head. 'Remember what?'

'You told me not to worry, that it happened all the time. You said that you'd had to clear up that awful morning of the doctor's death too. You told me that someone had walked mud through the farmhouse here. You thought it was strange, didn't you?' Cathy didn't wait for an answer. 'You wondered who had been out that early in the morning, or late the night before. But I think you probably knew, Jean. You had seen whose boots were damp in the hall. And no one's boots should have been damp unless the person they belonged to had been out walking or running on the moors. And why would anyone do that? One pair of boots, wasn't it, Jean? And in their panic on returning home and realising what they had done, they had dragged mud through the hallway, leaving you to clean it up before coming down to comfort me, having found the poor doctor at the bottom of Devil's Leap that next morning.'

Jean looked perplexed, but before she could speak there was a cry from the baby who, up until then, had been sleeping in Alison's arms. Alison turned to her husband and handed him the child.

'Take him for a minute,' she said. 'If you'll excuse me.' She began to walk to the door. Cathy stepped sideways to block her exit, but Alison was too fast and pushed her. She fell awkwardly, knocking her head on the side of the door and cried out in pain. But even in the commotion, she heard the front door slam and the sound of the Land Rover starting in the yard.

'Shit!' Cathy screamed, but both Iain and Ross were already chasing on foot, following the slippery path to the moors. Suzalinna helped Cathy up and together they watched from the doorway as the car bumped and jolted down the stony track.

'They'll never catch up. She's going to Devil's Leap,' Cathy cried. 'Oh God, what have I done?'

34

'I was willing you not to speak,' Cathy said, as they stood by the car.

'Oh God, well, I did wonder. The boots, you mean?' asked Jean.

'Yes. It was a bit of a long shot and hardly proof. I was afraid you'd say you hadn't been sure. Anyway, it was enough to force her into an admission.'

'What will happen to her?'

'I don't know.' She sighed. 'As I said, there wasn't any proof, just one note, and I think that even if the police did decide to take further action, any court would throw the case out. She needs psychiatric help rather than punishment.'

'Poor Iain,' Jean said, shaking her head. 'He'll struggle to manage. Thank God they stopped her.'

'But I still don't understand how it came about,' cut in Suzalinna, who stood by the front door holding the last of Cathy's bags. 'Was it just chance her marrying Iain and coming back to settle here, or was that all planned too?'

'Oh goodness, no. Well, I don't imagine so. Jean, your mum

said that the husband, Mr McCabe, broke down after the death of his wife. He was so distraught that he was barely able to care for himself, let alone his surviving daughter. She was put up for adoption.'

'So, Alison was adopted? So that wasn't her birth mother at the funeral then. I spoke to her in the pub,' Jean said. 'She was lovely.'

'She was lovely. I met her too. No, she wasn't Alison's birth mother. She gave that away when I chatted briefly with her. She told me that she had never expected to be a mother, let alone a grandmother. It did make me wonder. I think that probably, Alison had a very happy childhood. I wonder if she even remembered her first few years. I think it is customary to have a child adopted away from the area where they have lived before. Alison was raised in Perth, some sixty miles away.' Cathy smiled. 'Perhaps her adoptive mother knew of the story. Maybe she knew the reason for her adoption, perhaps not. It was complete chance that she met and fell for Iain. Even he had been out of Kinnaven a long time and only returned to help with the farm.' Cathy looked at her two friends. 'Lots of coincidences,' she said.

'My mum wouldn't call that coincidence,' Jean said, and Cathy smiled.

'The draw of the place, you mean? Yes, it does seem to have that quality, doesn't it? Both Devil's Leap and Kinnaven as a whole. I've felt it myself.' Cathy felt her cheeks redden. 'Anyway,' she continued, 'I wonder if at times Alison did have small flashes of recollection as she went about her business in the village. She must have been only four or five when she left but I think children do remember things quite well. I had an idea that the McCabe family might actually have lived in the cottage I was staying in. I remember when I first arrived, Alison went to walk through a doorway that didn't exist. She seemed a little flustered and said there should be a door there. Her father had been a farm labourer so it isn't inconceivable.

'For a short while, I worried that Alison might have had a grudge against the old farmer if he had been her father's employer, and this might have been a reason to kill him too. But I was relieved to hear from the hospital that he had died of natural causes. I hate to think of Alison being so vindictive as that. I'll never know what started her up on her vendetta against the doctor though. I think the old doctor might have given herself away. If Alison had gone to see her, especially if it was with her newborn baby, or even while she was pregnant, the doctor might well have seen a similarity. It must have been a shock. Dr Cosgrove was possibly already in a fragile state considering her retirement and then, to have this sudden and unexpected reminder of a case she had tried so hard to forget, well, it must have been dreadful.

'I wouldn't be surprised if Alison's strange recollections of the place, coupled with the doctor's reaction on seeing her, made her ask questions. Her adoptive mother would have been the person to start with. The rest would have been simple. On confirming that she had been Andrea's daughter, she decided to seek her revenge. Imagine living in that farmhouse knowing that you were so close to where your mother had killed herself. And in the village still, going about her business, was the woman who had caused it. It must have been torture.'

'Having her own baby at the time, what with all of this going on, must have sent her over the edge,' Suzalinna said. 'Postnatal psychosis? I guess psychiatry will sort it all out anyway.'

'Thank goodness it's over.' Jean sighed, and reaching out, she clumsily hugged Cathy. 'I'll miss you, you know? Thank you for everything.'

They got in the car. It had been arranged that Saj would

return next week to collect Cathy's car. She was still too drowsy to safely drive and, even if she had been capable, she doubted that Suzalinna would have allowed it. Her friend's car crept forward and they waved. They took the bumpy track up and past the farmhouse. Suzalinna slowed and stopped. Cathy wound down the window to speak to him.

'That you away?' Ross asked. 'Listen, I'm sorry if I was rude or messed you around. I didn't mean to...'

'Honestly, I should thank you. You shook me up a bit and I'm grateful for that. More than you can know.'

Ross looked at the ground.

'I take it you're not going to sell up? It would seem a shame to break up the land.'

Ross smiled. 'I suppose someone has to help run the place and I'll get the hang of it soon enough until Iain can manage or find someone else.'

'I'm pleased. And the other small matter?'

Ross grimaced.

'If you're going to win her back, you've got a lot of grovelling to do. I think the best way to show her that you've changed is to go up to Aberdeen as soon as you can and buy back the doctor's jewellery. I assume you went to a pawnshop? You have the money now, surely. I hear some second-cousin is coming up next week to sort the doctor's house. Get it returned by then and no one needs to know.'

Ross nodded. 'It was my idea. Jean went along with it. I took advantage of her.'

Cathy smiled slightly. 'I don't suppose you can return the money you took from the surgery too? I assume that was why Dr Cosgrove spoke to you before she died? Maybe leave them a donation as an apology. I think that might go down rather well. Oh, and Ross? Fatherhood will suit you, by the way.'

'Calum, you mean? He's a good kid.'

Cathy smiled. 'I think you and Jean need to talk. She must be at least eight weeks and I assume the baby's yours.'

They drove away; the car snaking up the country roads to meet the main route to the south. Cathy watched his figure in the wing mirror until they turned the corner. He stood with his hands on his hips, shaking his head.

She waited for it and when her friend finally spoke, she turned and laughed.

'Cathy Moreland!' Suzalinna said. 'Are you telling me that this entire time I've been worrying about you being lonely and unstable, you've done all this? It seems like you've unearthed every secret going in the place!'

Cathy grinned.

The car came to the crest of the hill and for a moment or two, the position allowed them to gaze on the village of Kinnaven below, sweeping down to the cliffs and out to sea. Poor Dr Cosgrove. Cathy knew that in choosing death, she had put an end to the hurt that the village had long endured. Her self-sacrifice had been a parting gesture to a community she had served so long and loved. Not only this, but she had inadvertently saved Cathy as well. Still, the terrible consequences for those dealing with the fall out could not be forgotten. Cathy thought of the practice the old doctor had left behind, her GP partner, who would probably always feel guilt for not having spotted the warning signs. And then there were the police and rescue workers who had lifted her from the shore. No, Cathy considered. If anything, Dr Cosgrove had set the whole cycle of pain into motion once more and a further generation of Kinnaven residents might be haunted by what they had witnessed.

'Pretty as a picture,' Suzalinna said, and Cathy thought of

him then, the solitary man living on the clifftops in his ramshackle house. The artist who had spent his life painting and re-painting the same seascape, embittered but empowered by his loneliness.

'I wonder,' Cathy said to herself. But when her friend glanced at her, she had turned away.

35

It was three weeks to the day since she left Kinnaven. She had been into the practice the previous morning to have coffee with the other doctors. All were pleased to see her looking so much more like her old self, and even better and more rejuvenated than before, her senior partner, James, had commented. It would take time, of course, but she knew she was on the right track.

She had been ensconced in daytime television when it arrived and was still dressed in her pyjamas and a fleece cardigan. The parcel had been packaged wisely, with the address written on a full envelope, neatly attached to the front with tape. She carefully peeled off the envelope and, placing the parcel to one side, opened it and read the meticulous, spidery hand.

Dear Doctor Moreland,

I hope that this letter finds you well and your patients are appreciative of your return. I do hope that your stay in Kinnaven was enjoyable.

Forgive me for writing when we are but the briefest of acquaintances, but I feel that I owe you, of all people, an explanation. My time here is short and I hope that when you read this, if it has been forwarded to you as I have directed my solicitors, I will, in fact, be dead. It amuses me to think of myself, perhaps looking down on you now.

It may surprise you to know that you were the first visitor I had had in over twenty years. That statement may shock you and you may ask yourself why, but I deliberately chose this life. Now, nearing death, I feel that I must leave an explanation for my behaviour. An epitaph, if you will.

I believe fate brought us together on the cliffs all those weeks ago. You won't believe in such a notion, but tolerate an old man's fancies for a moment or two and allow me to explain.

You may, or may not know, of Kinnaven's history, and don't worry, I will not bore you with this for long. It was an ex-fishing town, although how the men raised their rewards from the sea and up the rugged cliff-paths is beyond my comprehension. My parents settled here. I, along with my siblings, all of whom are now deceased, enjoyed, in many ways, an idyllic childhood. And, finding my calling in art, I chose to stay on. I'm sure that even to the untrained eye, anyone can appreciate the endless inspiration the coastline has to offer. Rarely was there a day in my life when I couldn't see a change of luminosity in the sky or a new depth to the sea that I hadn't before witnessed. But you must forgive me as I digress. The subject is, you understand, dear to me.

Art almost predisposes a person to lead a reclusive existence. Throughout my youth, I had no interest in an attachment with anyone. I was content in my own company and although it may seem odd to you, I led a full and meaningful life. I must admit that my work at the time was appalling in quality. Perhaps I had lost insight or motivation. That was until I met her... I apologise for this part in the story, doctor. I hope that morally, you are not offended by what I am about to write, but what we had was almost indescribable.

She was married and she too, like you all these years later, found me painting on the clifftops. Fate, you see? It was an instantaneous love for both of us, I am unashamed to say. I had no interest in hearing about her husband or her other child and she spoke little of them when we were together. We were consumed completely by our love. My work took on a remarkable quality at the time. Even I was awestruck by the magnificence of some of the pieces I produced during our affair.

It ended. She was pregnant and the child was mine. I urged her to leave her husband and family and to move in with me, but she had more integrity than I and ended our attachment. I saw her only once after the child was born. It was a girl and she brought her to me. I cannot begin to express my depth of feeling for that child, even in the few moments that I held her. Again, I urged her to leave her husband and promised her a new life away from Kinnaven, where we could bring up the child and be free from the humdrum of ordinary existence that she endured. You understand, doctor? She was an extraordinary person. She refused, of course. I could see she was unhappy. She said as much in the letters she wrote. She had arranged to see our local doctor. Her mood had become so low it was pitiful. I was relieved that she was seeking help. I hoped that the doctor would offer support.

It pains me to even write the woman's name down, but the doctor, Dr Cosgrove, could not have been less sympathetic. She failed to understand the depth of her despair and, when she explained our situation in confidence, the doctor insinuated that it had been immoral!

In the early hours of the following morning, the woman who had stolen my heart for eternity fell from the cliffs. With her, she took our daughter.

Dr Moreland, I am sure in your dealings with grieving relatives, you will have seen a variety of emotions. I doubt, however, that you will begin to comprehend the utter torture of my existence following their deaths. Unable to display grief or even attend their funeral up at the church for fear of being noticed by her husband, I mourned alone. I disconnected from the rest of the world.

My work stopped for some time and I hid, scarred and beaten by life's cruelty. That was until I found a reason to live again, and that reason, absurd as it may sound, was my imminent death. Oh, with what vigour I have welcomed it. And the doctor? It gratifies me in many ways that she chose the same way to die as my beloved. I think her choice to fall from the clifftops indulged me more than you can imagine.

And now, as my time is short, I leave you this gift. I was touched by your concern, you see? A concern, and gentleness that I had not felt in near-on thirty years. I thank you for showing it to me and reminding me of it, and her.

I am yours, most sincerely,

Alexander Buchannan

Cathy opened the parcel. She held it up. The painting that had transfixed her when she had visited his house. But, as she brought it closer, she could see he had added a small detail that had not been there originally. On the clifftops was the figure of a woman, her hair blowing freely in the wind.

THE END

ACKNOWLEDGEMENTS

Many thanks to Tara, Clare and Betsy from Bloodhound. You have been hugely supportive throughout and have made the publishing process straightforward and incredibly enjoyable.

Thanks also to my beloved husband for putting up with it all and my son, for his comical suggestions throughout the writing stage! To my parents also, I thank you for your encouragement and support.

Finally, thank you to my readers for picking up the book. I can't wait to share more stories about Dr Cathy Moreland with you!

A NOTE FROM THE PUBLISHER

Thank you for reading this book. If you enjoyed it please do consider leaving a review on Amazon to help others find it too.

We hate typos. All of our books have been rigorously edited and proofread, but sometimes mistakes do slip through. If you have spotted a typo, please do let us know and we can get it amended within hours.

info@bloodhoundbooks.com